The Kreutzer Sonata

LEO TOLSTOY

The Kreutzer Sonata

Translated by DAVID MCDUFF

GREAT LOVES

PENGUIN BOOKS

Published by the Penguin Group
Penguin Books Ltd, 80 Strand, London WC2R ORL, England
Penguin Group (USA) Inc., 375 Hudson Street, New York, New York 10014, USA
Penguin Group (Canada), 90 Eglinton Avenue East, Suite 700, Toronto, Ontario, Canada M4P 2Y3
(a division of Pearson Penguin Canada Inc.)
Penguin Ireland, 25 St Stephen's Green, Dublin 2, Ireland
(a division of Penguin Books Ltd)
Penguin Group (Australia), 250 Camberwell Road, Camberwell, Victoria 3124, Australia
(a division of Pearson Australia Group Pty Ltd)
Penguin Books India Pvt Ltd, 11 Community Centre, Panchsheel Park, New Delhi – 110 017, India
Penguin Group (NZ), 67 Apollo Drive, Rosedale, North Shore 0632, New Zealand
(a division of Pearson New Zealand Ltd)
Penguin Books (South Africa) (Pty) Ltd, 24 Sturdee Avenue,
Rosebank, Johannesburg 2196, South Africa

Penguin Books Ltd, Registered Offices: 80 Strand, London WC2R ORL, England

www.penguin.com

This translation first published in *The Kreutzer Sonata and Other Stories* by Penguin Books 1983
This edition published in Penguin Books 2007

1

Translation copyright © David Duff, 1985, 2004
All rights reserved

Typeset by Rowland Phototypesetting Ltd, Bury St Edmunds, Suffolk
Printed in England by Clays Ltd, St Ives plc

978-0-141-03481-2

Count Leo Nikolayevich Tolstoy (1828–1910) was born in Tula province, Russia. He studied Oriental languages and law at the University of Kazan, then led a life of pleasure until 1851 when he joined an artillery regiment in the Caucasus and subsequently took part in the Crimean War. He married Sofya Andreyevna Behrs in 1862 and together they had thirteen children.

Tolstoy is widely regarded as one of the greatest of all novelists, particularly noted for *War and Peace* (1865–1868) and *Anna Karenina* (1874–1876); masterpieces in their scope, breadth and realistic depiction of Russian life. *The Kreutzer Sonata* is the self-lacerating confession of a man consumed by sexual jealousy. The story caused a sensation when it first appeared, and Tolstoy's wife was appalled that he had drawn on their own experiences together to create a scathing indictment of marriage.

The Kreutzer Sonata

But I say unto you, That whosoever
looketh on a woman to lust after her
hath committed adultery with her
already in his heart.

(Matthew v, 28)

His disciples say unto him, If the case of the man be
so with his wife, it is not good to marry.

But he said unto them, All men cannot receive this
saying, save they to whom it is given.

For there are some eunuchs, which were so born
from their mother's womb: and there are some
eunuchs, which were made eunuchs of men: and
there be eunuchs, which have made themselves
eunuchs for the kingdom of heaven's sake. He that
is able to receive it, let him receive it.

(Matthew xix, 10–12)

I

This took place in early spring. It was the second uninterrupted day of our journey. Every so often passengers who were only going short distances would enter the railway carriage and leave it again, but there were three people who, like myself, had boarded the train at its point of origin and were still travelling: a plain, elderly lady with an exhausted-looking face, who was smoking cigarettes and was dressed in a hat and coat that might almost have been those of a man; her companion, a talkative man of about forty, with trim, new luggage; and another man who was rather small of stature and whose movements were nervous and jerky – he was not yet old, but his curly hair had obviously turned grey prematurely, and his eyes had a peculiar light in them as they flickered from one object to another. He was dressed in an old coat that looked as though it might have been made by an expensive tailor; it had a lambskin collar, and he wore a tall cap of the same material. Whenever he unfastened his coat, a long-waisted jacket and a Russian embroidered shirt came into view. Another peculiar thing about this man was that every now and again he uttered strange sounds, as if he were clearing his throat or beginning to laugh, but breaking off in silence.

Throughout the entire duration of the journey this

man studiously avoided talking to any of the other passengers or becoming acquainted with them. If anyone spoke to him he would reply curtly and abruptly; he spent the time reading, looking out of the window, smoking or taking from his old travelling-bag the provisions he had brought with him and then sipping tea or munching a snack.

I had the feeling that his solitude was weighing him down, and I tried several times to engage him in conversation. Each time our eyes met, however, which was frequently, as we were sitting obliquely opposite one another, he would turn away and start reading his book or gazing out of the window.

Shortly before evening on that second day, the train stopped at a large station, and the nervous man stepped outside, fetched some boiling water and made tea for himself. The man with the smart luggage, a lawyer, as I later discovered, went to have a glass of tea in the station buffet with his travelling companion, the cigarette-smoking lady in the man's coat.

During their absence several new passengers entered the carriage. They included a tall, clean-shaven old man whose face was creased all over in wrinkles; he was evidently a merchant, and he wore a polecat fur coat and a cloth cap that had an enormous peak. He sat down opposite the places temporarily vacated by the lawyer and the lady, and immediately launched into a conversation with a young man who looked like a salesclerk and who had also entered the carriage at this station.

My seat was diagonally opposite theirs, and since

the train was not in motion I could, when no one was passing down the carriage, overhear snatches of what they were saying. The merchant started off by telling the other man that he was on his way to visit his estate, which lay just one stop down the line; then, as such men always do, they began to discuss trade and prices, the current state of the Moscow market, and eventually, as always, they arrived at the subject of the Nizhny Novgorod summer fair. The salesclerk embarked on a description of the drinking and antics of a certain rich merchant they both knew, but the old man would not hear him out; instead, he began to talk about the jamborees he himself had taken part in at Kunavino in days gone by. Of his role in these he was evidently proud, and it was with open delight that he related how once, when he and this same mutual acquaintance had been drunk together in Kunavino, they had got up to some mischief of a kind that he could only describe in whispers. The salesclerk's guffaw filled the entire carriage, and the old man laughed along with him, exposing a couple of yellow teeth to view.

Not expecting to hear anything of interest, I rose and left my seat with the aim of taking a stroll along the platform until it was time for the train to depart. In the doorway I bumped into the lawyer and the lady, who were chattering animatedly to one another as they found their way back to their seats.

'You won't have time,' the talkative lawyer said to me. 'The second bell's going to go any minute now.'

And so it was: before I had even reached the end of the line of carriages the bell rang. When I got back to my seat I found the lawyer and the lady deep in energetic conversation. The old merchant sat opposite them in silence, looking severely in front of him and chewing his teeth from time to time in disapproval.

'So then she just told her husband straight out,' the lawyer was saying with a smile as I made my way past him. 'She said she couldn't and wouldn't live with him any more, because . . .'

And he began to say something else, something I could not make out. More passengers came trooping in behind me; then the guard walked down the carriage, followed by a porter in a tremendous hurry, and for quite a long time there ensued such an uproar that no conversation could possibly be heard. When things had quietened down again and I could once more hear the lawyer's voice, the conversation had evidently passed from the particular to the general.

The lawyer was saying that the question of divorce was very much the object of public discussion in Europe just now, and that cases of this type were cropping up in our own country with an ever-increasing degree of frequency. Noticing that his voice had become the only one in the carriage, the lawyer cut short his homily and turned to the old man.

'There was none of that sort of thing in the old days, was there?' he said, smiling affably.

The old man was about to reply, but at that moment the train began to move and, taking off his cap, he began crossing himself and reciting a prayer in a whisper. The lawyer waited politely, averting his gaze. When he had finished his prayer and his thrice-repeated crossing of himself, the old man put his cap fairly and squarely back on his head, rearranged himself in his seat, and began to speak.

'Oh there was, sir. It's just that there wasn't so much of it, that's all,' he said. 'You can't expect anything else nowadays. They've all gotten that well educated.'

As the train began to gather speed it kept rattling over points, and it was not easy to hear what he was saying. I was interested, however, and I shifted my seat so as to be closer to him. The interest of my neighbour, the nervous man with the light in his eyes, had also plainly been aroused, and he continued to listen while staying where he was.

'But what's wrong with education?' said the lady, with a scarcely perceptible smile. 'Was it really better to get married in the old way, with the bride and bridegroom never even setting eyes on one another beforehand?' she continued, replying, as many women do, not to what the person she was addressing had actually said, but to what she thought he was going to say. 'You didn't know whether you were even going to like the man, let alone whether you'd be able to love him; you got married to the first man who came along and spent all the rest of your life in misery. Do you think that was better?' she said, making it clear that her words were addressed primarily to the lawyer and myself, and only in the last instance to the old man with whom she was talking.

'They've all gotten that well educated,' repeated the old merchant, surveying the lady contemptuously and letting her question go unanswered.

'I'd like to hear you explain the connection you see between education and marital discord,' the lawyer said, with a faint smile.

The merchant was about to say something, but the lady cut in before him.

'No, those days have gone,' she said. But the lawyer would not allow her to continue.

'Just a moment, let him say what's on his mind.'

'Education leads to nothing but a lot of silliness,' said the old man, firmly.

'People who don't love one another are forced to get married, and then everyone wonders why they can't live in harmony together,' said the lady hurriedly, turning an appraising eye on the lawyer, myself and even on the salesclerk, who had risen out of his seat and was leaning his elbows on its back, listening to the conversation with a smile. 'After all, it's only animals that can be mated at their masters' will; human beings have inclinations and attachments of their own,' she went on, apparently from a desire to say something wounding to the merchant.

'You're wrong there, missus,' said the old man. 'The true difference is that an animal's just an animal, but human beings have been given a law to live by.'

'Very well, but how are you supposed to live with someone you don't love?' asked the lady, still in a hurry to express her opinions, which doubtless seemed brand-new to her.

'People didn't make such a fuss about all that in the old days,' said the merchant in a serious voice. 'That's all just come in lately. First thing you hear her say nowadays is "I'm leaving you." It's a fashion that's caught on even among the muzhiks. "Here you are," she says; "here's your shirts and trousers, I'm off with Vanka, his hair's curlier than yours." And it's no good arguing with her. Whereas what ought to come first for a woman is fear.'

The salesclerk looked first at the lawyer, then at the lady, and finally at me; he was only just keeping back a smile, and was preparing to treat what the merchant had said with either ridicule or approval, according to how it went down.

'What sort of fear?' asked the lady.

'Fear of her *hu-u-u*sband, of course. That kind of fear.'

'Well, my dear man, those days have gone, I'm afraid,' said the lady, with an edge of malice in her voice.

'No, missus, those days can never be gone. Eve, the woman, was created from the rib of man, and so she will remain until the end of time,' said the old man, with such a stern and triumphant shake of his head that the salesclerk at once decided that victory was on the side of the merchant, and he burst into loud laughter.

'That's only the way you menfolk see it,' said the lady, not ceding defeat, and giving us all an appraising look. 'You've granted yourselves freedom, but you want to keep women locked up in a tower. Meanwhile you've decided you're going to allow yourselves anything you want.'

'No one's decided anything of the kind. It's just that

a home profits nothing from a man's endeavours, and a woman is a fragile vessel,' the merchant continued earnestly.

The merchant's solemn, earnest tone of voice was evidently having a persuasive effect on his audience. Even the lady appeared to have had some of the wind taken out of her sails, though she showed no sign of giving up the struggle.

'Yes, well, but I think you would agree that a woman is a human being, and that she has feelings just as a man has, wouldn't you? So what's she supposed to do if she doesn't love her husband?'

'If she doesn't love him?' echoed the merchant darkly, making a grimace with his lips and eyebrows. 'She'd better love him.'

The salesclerk seemed to find this line of argument particularly attractive, and he made a noise of approval.

'Oh, no she hadn't,' said the lady. 'If there's no love there in the first place, you can't force it.'

'And what if the wife's unfaithful to the husband?' asked the lawyer.

'That mustn't happen,' said the old man. 'You have to be on the look-out for that kind of thing.'

'But what if it does happen? It does, after all.'

'There's some as it happens to, but not the likes of us,' said the old man.

No one ventured anything for a while. The salesclerk shifted a little closer. Apparently not wishing to be left out of things, he gave a smile and said: 'Oh, but it does, you know. There was a scandal with one of our lads. It wasn't easy to tell whose fault it was, either.

Married a loose woman, he did. She started her flirting around, but he was the homely type, and he had a bit of education. First jump she had was with one of the clerks in the office. The lad tried to make her see reason, but there was no stopping her. All kinds of filthy tricks she got up to. Started stealing his money. So he beat her. Didn't do any good, she just went from bad to worse. She started playing around – if you'll pardon the expression – with a heathen, a Jew he was. What was the lad supposed to do? He threw her out. Now he lives as a bachelor, and she walks the streets.'

'So he was an idiot,' said the old man. 'If he'd never given her any leeway in the first place but had kept her properly reined in, she'd no doubt still be living with him to this day. You mustn't allow them any freedom from the word go. Never trust a horse in the paddock or a wife in the home.'

At this moment the guard arrived to take the tickets for the next station. The old man gave up his ticket.

'Yes, you have to rein them in early on, those womenfolk, otherwise it all goes to pot.'

'But what about that story you were telling us just then about those married men going on the spree in Kunavino?' I could not resist asking.

'That's something altogether different,' said the merchant, and lapsed into silence.

When the whistle blew he got up, fetched his travelling-bag from under his seat, drew his overcoat tightly around him and, raising his cap to us, went out on the brake platform.

2

As soon as the old man had gone, several voices took up the conversation again.

'That fellow was straight out of the Old Testament,' said the salesclerk.

'A veritable walking *Domostroy*,' said the lady. 'What a barbarous conception of woman and marriage!'

'Yes, we're a long way behind the European idea of marriage,' said the lawyer.

'What these people don't seem to understand,' said the lady, 'is that marriage without love isn't marriage at all; love is the only thing that can sanctify a marriage, and the only true marriages are those that are sanctified by love.'

The salesclerk listened, smiling. He was trying to memorize as much of this clever talk as he could, for use on future occasions.

The lady's homily was interrupted half-way through by a sound that seemed to come from behind me and might have been a broken laugh or a sob. When we turned round, we saw my neighbour, the solitary, grey-haired man with the light in his eyes; he had evidently become interested in our conversation and had come closer to us without our noticing. He was standing up, his hands leaning on the back of his seat, and he was plainly in a state of great agitation. His face was red, and a muscle in one of his cheeks was twitching.

'What's this love . . . love . . . love . . . that sanctifies marriage?' he stammered.

Observing the state of agitation he was in, the lady tried to make her reply as gentle and thorough as possible.

'True love . . . if true love exists between a man and a woman, then marriage, too, is possible,' said the lady.

'Yes, but what's true love?' said the man with the light in his eyes, smiling timidly and awkwardly.

'Everybody knows what love is,' said the lady, visibly anxious to bring this conversation to an end.

'I don't,' said the man. 'You'd have to define what you mean . . .'

'What? It's very simple,' said the lady, though she had to think for a moment. 'Love? Love is the exclusive preference for one man or one woman above all others,' she said.

'A preference lasting how long? A month? Two days, half an hour?' said the grey-haired man, and he gave a laugh.

'No, not that kind of preference, you're talking about something else.'

'What she means,' said the lawyer, intervening and designating the lady, 'is firstly that marriage ought to be based primarily on affection – love, if you like – and that only if this is present does marriage offer something that is, as it were, sacred. Secondly, that no marriage which is not based on natural affection – love, if you like – carries with it any moral obligation. Have I understood you correctly?' he asked, turning to the lady.

By a movement of her head, the lady indicated her approval of this exposition of her views.

'It follows, therefore . . .' the lawyer began, pursuing his discourse. But by this time the nervous man, whose eyes were now on fire, was clearly restraining himself only with difficulty.

Without waiting for the lawyer to conclude, he said: 'Yes, that's exactly what I'm talking about, the preference for one man or one woman above all others, but what I'm asking is: a preference for how long?'

'How long? A long time, sometimes for as long as one lives,' said the lady, shrugging her shoulders.

'But that only happens in novels, not in real life. In real life a preference like that lasts maybe a year, but that's very rare; more often it's a few months, or weeks, or days, or hours,' he said, evidently aware that this opinion would shock everyone, and pleased at the result.

'What are you saying? No, no! Sorry, but no!' we all three of us burst out together. Even the salesclerk made a noise of disapproval.

'I know, I know,' said the grey-haired man in a raised voice, louder than any of us. 'You're talking about the way things are supposed to be, but I'm talking about the way things actually are. Every man experiences what you call love each time he meets a pretty woman.'

'Oh, but what you're saying is dreadful! Surely there's an emotion that exists between people called love, a feeling that lasts not just months or years, but for the whole of their lives?'

'Definitely not. Even if one admits that a man may prefer a certain woman all his life, it's more than probable that the woman will prefer someone else. That's the way it's always been and that's the way it still is,' he said, taking a cigarette from his cigarette case and lighting it.

'But there can be mutual affection, surely,' said the lawyer.

'No, there can't,' the grey-haired man retorted, 'any more than two marked peas can turn up next to one another in a pea-cart. And besides, it's not just a question of probability, but of having too much of a good thing. Loving the same man or woman all your life – why, that's like supposing the same candle could last you all your life,' he said, inhaling greedily.

'But you're just talking about physical love. Wouldn't you admit that there can be a love that's founded on shared ideals, on spiritual affinity?'

'Spiritual affinity? Shared ideals?' he repeated, making his sound again. 'There's not much point in going to bed together if that's what you're after (excuse the plain language). Do people go to bed with one another because of shared ideals?' he said, laughing nervously.

'I'm sorry,' said the lawyer. 'The facts contradict what you're saying. Our own eyes tell us that marriages exist, that the whole of humanity or at least the greater part of it lives in a married state and that a lot of people manage to stay decently married for rather a long time.'

The grey-haired man began to laugh again. 'First you tell me that marriage is founded on love, and then when I express my doubts as to the existence of any love apart from the physical kind you try to prove its existence by the fact that marriages exist. But marriage nowadays is just a deception!'

'No, sir, with respect,' said the lawyer. 'All I said was that marriages have existed and that they continue to exist.'

'All right, so they exist. But why? They've existed and they continue to exist for the sort of people who see in marriage something that's sacred, a sacrament that binds them in the eyes of God. Marriages exist for those people, but not for the likes of you and me. Our sort enter into a marriage without seeing in it anything except copulation, and it usually ends either in infidelity or violence. Infidelity is easier to put up with. The husband and wife simply pretend to everyone that they're living in monogamy, when in actual fact they're living in polygamy and polyandry. It's not very pretty, but it's feasible. But when, as is most often the case, the husband and wife accept the external obligation to live together all their lives and have, by the second month, come to loathe the sight of each other, want to get divorced and yet go on living together, it usually ends in that terrible hell that drives them to drink, makes them shoot themselves, kill and poison each other,' he said, speaking faster and faster, not letting anyone else get a word in, and growing hotter and hotter under the collar. No one said anything. We all felt too embarrassed.

'Yes, there's no doubt that married life has its critical episodes,' said the lawyer, endeavouring to bring to an end a conversation that had grown more heated than was seemly.

'I can see you've recognized me,' said the grey-haired man quietly, trying to appear unruffled.

'No, I don't think I have the pleasure . . .'

'It's not much of a pleasure. Pozdnyshev's the name. I'm the fellow who had one of those critical episodes you were talking about. So critical was it, in fact, that I ended up murdering my wife,' he said, making his noise again. 'Oh, I say, I'm sorry. Er . . . I didn't mean to embarrass you.'

'Not at all, for heaven's sake . . .' said the lawyer, not quite sure himself what he meant by this 'for heaven's sake'.

But Pozdnyshev, who was not paying any attention to him, turned round sharply and went back to his seat. The lawyer and the lady whispered to one another. I was sitting beside Pozdnyshev and I kept quiet, not knowing what to say. It was too dark to read, so I closed my eyes and pretended I wanted to go to sleep. We continued in this silent fashion until the train reached the next station.

While the train was at a standstill, the lawyer and the lady moved along to another carriage as they had arranged to do earlier on with the guard. The salesclerk made himself comfortable on the empty seat and went to sleep. As for Pozdnyshev, he continued to smoke cigarettes and sip the tea he had made for himself at the previous station.

When I opened my eyes and looked at him, he suddenly turned to me with an air of resolve and exasperation: 'I think perhaps you're finding it unpleasant to sit next to me, since you know who I am? If that's so, I'll move.'

'Oh, no, please don't.'

'Well, would you like some tea, then? It's strong, mind.' He poured me a glass of tea. 'What they were saying . . . It's all wrong, you know . . .'

'What are you talking about?' I asked.

'Oh, the same thing – that love they keep going on about, and what it really is. You're sure you'd not rather be getting some sleep?'

'Quite sure.'

'Well then, if you like, I'll tell you how that love of theirs drove me to the point where I did what I did.'

'By all means, if it's not too painful for you.'

'No, it's keeping quiet about it that's the painful part. Have some more. Or is it too strong for you?'

The tea was the colour of tar, but I swilled down a glass of it all the same. Just then the guard passed down the carriage. Pozdnyshev followed him angrily with his gaze and did not start speaking again until he was gone.

3

'Very well, then, I'll tell you . . . You're absolutely sure you want me to?'

I repeated that I did, very much. He said nothing for a moment. Then, rubbing his face in his hands, he began: 'If I'm going to tell you, I'll have to start at the beginning, and tell you how and why I got married, and what I was like before my marriage.

'Before my marriage I lived the sort of life all men do, in our social circle, that is. I'm a landowner, I've got a university degree, and I used to be a marshal of nobility. As I say, I lived the sort of life all men do – a life of debauchery. And, like all the men of our class, I thought that this debauched existence was perfectly proper. I considered myself a charming young man, a thoroughly moral sort of fellow. I wasn't a seducer, had no unnatural tastes, and didn't make debauchery into my main aim in life, as many young men of my age did, but indulged in it with decency and moderation, for the sake of my health. I avoided women who might have succeeded in tying me down by having babies or forming attachments to me. Actually, there probably were both babies and attachments, but I behaved as if there weren't. Not only did I regard this as moral behaviour – I was proud of it.'

He paused and made his sound, as he apparently did whenever some new idea occurred to him.

'And that's the really loathsome thing about it,' he exclaimed. 'Debauchery isn't something physical. Not even the most outrageous physicality can be equated with debauchery. Debauchery – real debauchery – takes place when you free yourself from any moral regard for the woman you enter into physical relations with. But you see, I made the acquisition of that freedom into a matter of personal honour. I remember the agony of mind I once went through when I was in too much of a hurry to remember to pay a woman who had probably fallen in love with me and had let me go to bed with her. I just couldn't rest easy until I'd sent her the money, thereby demonstrating that I didn't consider myself morally obliged towards her in any way. Don't sit there nodding your head as if you agreed with me!' he suddenly shouted at me. 'I know what you're thinking! You're all the same, you too, unless you're a rare exception, you see things the way I did then. Oh I say, forget that, I'm sorry,' he continued. 'But the fact is that it's horrible, horrible, horrible!'

'What is?' I inquired.

'The abyss of error we live in regarding women and our relations with them. It's no good, I just can't talk calmly about it. It's not merely because of that episode, as the other gentleman called it, but because ever since I went through it my eyes have been opened and I've seen everything in a completely new light. Everything's been turned inside out, it's all inside out! . . .'

He lit a cigarette and, leaning forward with his elbows on his knees, began to tell me his story.

It was so dark that I could not see his face, only hear his forceful, pleasant voice raised above the rattling and swaying of the carriage.

4

'Yes, it was only after the suffering I endured, only thanks to it that I came to understand what the root of the trouble was, saw the way things ought to be, and thus obtained an insight into the horror of things the way they were.

'If you want to know, this is how and when it all began, the sequence of events that led up to that episode of mine. It started shortly before my sixteenth birthday. I was still at grammar school then. My older brother was a first-year student at university. As yet I had no experience of women, but like all the wretched boys of our social class I was no longer innocent. For more than a year I'd been exposed to the corrupting influence of the other boys. Woman – not any woman in particular but woman as a sweet, ineffable presence – woman, any woman, the nakedness of woman already tormented me. The hours I spent alone were not pure ones. I suffered in the way ninety-nine per cent of our youngsters suffer. I was horrified – I suffered, prayed, and succumbed. I was already corrupted, both in my imagination and in reality, but I had still not taken the final step. In my lonely way I was going from bad to worse, but so far I had not laid my hands on any other human being. But then one of my brother's friends, a student, a *bon vivant*, one of those so-called "jolly good chaps" (an out-and-out villain, in other words), who had taught us to play cards and drink vodka, persuaded us to go with him to a certain place after a drinking-bout one evening. My brother was still a virgin, like myself, and he fell that very same night. And I, a fifteen-year-old boy, defiled myself and contributed to the defilement of a woman without the slightest understanding of what I was doing. After all, never once had I heard any of my elders say that what I was doing was wrong. And it's not something you hear said nowadays, either. It's true that it's in the Ten Commandments, but you know as well as I do that they're only useful for giving the school chaplain the right answers on examination day, and even then they're not a great deal of help – much less so, for example, than knowing when to use *ut* in conditional clauses.

'That's the way it was: none of the older people whose opinions I respected ever told me that what I was doing was wrong. On the contrary, the people I looked up to told me it was the right thing to do. I was told that, after I had done it, my struggles and sufferings would ease. I was told this, and I read it. My elders assured me that it would be good for my health. As for my companions, they said it entailed a kind of merit, a certain bravado. Accordingly, I could see nothing but good in it. The danger of infection? But that, too, is taken care of. Our solicitous government takes pains to see to it. It supervises the orderly running of the licensed brothels and ensures the depravation of grammar-school boys. Even our doctors keep an eye on this problem, for a fee of course. That is only proper. They assert that debauchery is good for the health, for it's they who have instituted this form of tidy, legalized debauchery. I even know mothers who take an active concern for this aspect of their son's health. And science directs them to the brothels.'

'Why science?' I asked.

'What are doctors, if not the high priests of science? Who are the people responsible for depraving young lads, claiming it's essential for their health? They are. And having made such a claim, they proceed to apply their cures for syphilis with an air of the utmost gravity.'

'But why shouldn't they cure syphilis?'

'Because if even one per cent of the effort that is put into curing syphilis were to be employed in the eradication of debauchery, syphilis would long ago have disappeared from memory. But our efforts are employed not in eradicating debauchery, but in encouraging it, making it safe. Anyway that isn't the point. The point is that I, like nine out of ten, if not more, young men, not only in our own class but in all the others as well, even the peasantry, have had the horrible experience of falling without succumbing to the natural temptation of the charms of any one woman in particular. No, it wasn't a case of my being seduced by a woman. I fell because the society I lived in regarded what was a fall either as a bodily function that was both legitimate and necessary for the sake of health, or as a diversion that was thoroughly natural for a young man and was not only pardonable, but even innocent. I myself didn't know it was a fall; I simply began to indulge in something that was half pleasure and half physical necessity – both, I was assured, perfectly proper for young men of a certain age. I began to indulge in this debauchery in the same way as I began to drink and smoke. Yet there was something strangely moving about that first fall. I remember that immediately after it was over, right there in the room, I felt terribly, terribly sad; I wanted to weep, weep for my lost innocence, for my relation to women which had been forever spoiled, corrupted. Yes, the simple, natural relation I had had to women had been ruined for ever. From that day on I ceased to have a pure relation to women, nor was I any longer capable of one. I had become what is known as a fornicator. Being a fornicator is a physical condition similar to that of a morphine addict, an alcoholic or a smoker of opium. Just as a morphine addict, an alcoholic or a smoker of opium is no longer a normal individual, so a man who has had several women for the sake of his pleasure is no longer a normal person but one who has been spoiled for all time – a fornicator. And just as an alcoholic or a morphine addict can immediately be recognized by his features and physical mannerisms, so can a fornicator. A fornicator may restrain himself, struggle for self-control, but never again will his relation to women be simple, clear, pure, that of a brother to a sister. A fornicator can be instantly recognized by the intent look with which he examines a woman. I, too, became a fornicator and remained one, and that was my undoing.'

5

'Yes, that's how it happened. After that it got worse and worse; I became involved in all kinds of moral deviations. My God! I recoil in horror from the memory of all my filthy acts! I, whom all my friends used to laugh at because of what they called my innocence! And when one looks at our golden youth, at our officers, at those Parisians! And when all those gentlemen and myself, debauchees in our thirties with hundreds of the most varied and abominable crimes against women on our consciences, go into a drawing-room or a ballroom, well scrubbed, clean-shaven, perfumed, wearing immaculate linen, in evening dress or uniform, the very emblems of purity – aren't we a charming sight?

'Just give some thought for a moment to the way things ought to be and the way things actually are. This is the way things ought to be: when one of these gentlemen enters into relations with my sister or my daughter, I go up to him, take him aside and say to him quietly: "My dear fellow, I know the sort of life you lead, how you spend your nights and who you spend them with. This is no place for you. The girls in this house are pure and innocent. Be off with you!" That's how it ought to be. Now how things actually are is that when one of these gentlemen appears and starts dancing with my sister or my daughter, putting his arms round her, we rejoice, as long as he's rich and has connections. Always supposing, of course, that after Rigolboche he considers my daughter good enough for him. Even if there are consequences, an illness . . . it doesn't matter. They can cure anything nowadays. Good heavens, yes, I can think of several girls from the highest social circles whose parents enthusiastically married them off to syphilitics. Ugh, how vile! But the time will come when all that filth and deception will be shown for what it is!'

He made his strange sound several times and began to sip his tea. The tea was horribly strong, and there was no water with which to dilute it. I felt it was the two glasses of the stuff I had already drunk that were making me so agitated. The tea must also have been having an effect on him, for he was growing more and more excited. His voice was increasingly acquiring a singing, expressive quality. He shifted position constantly, now removing his hat, now putting it on again, and his face kept altering strangely in the semi-darkness where we sat.

'Well, and so that's the way I lived until I was thirty, without ever for one moment abandoning my intention of getting married and building for myself the most elevated and purest of family lives, and with that end in view I was keeping an eye out for a girl who might fill the bill,' he continued. 'I was wallowing in the slime of debauchery, and at the same time looking for girls who might be pure enough to be worthy of me! I rejected a lot of them because of that – because they weren't pure enough; but at last I found one whom I considered worthy of me. She was one of the two daughters of a Penza landowner who had once been very rich but had lost all his money.

'One evening after we'd been out boating and were going home together in the moonlight, I sat beside her and admired her curls and her shapely figure, hugged by the tight silk of the stockinet dress she was wearing. I suddenly decided that she was the one. That evening it seemed to me that she understood everything, all I was thinking and feeling, and that all my thoughts and feelings were of the most exalted kind. All it really was was that silk stockinet happened to suit her particularly well, as did curls, and that after a day spent close to her I wanted to get even closer.

'It's really quite remarkable how complete the illusion is that beauty is the same as goodness. A pretty woman may say the most stupid things, yet you listen, and you don't notice the stupidities, it all sounds so intelligent. She says and does things that are infamous, yet to you they seem delightful. And when at last she says something that is neither stupid nor infamous, as long as she's pretty, you're immediately convinced that she's quite wonderfully intelligent and of the very highest morality.

'I returned home positively beside myself with enthusiasm and decided that she was the acme of moral perfection and consequently worthy of being my wife. I proposed to her the very next day.

'What a tangled mess it all is! Out of a thousand men who get married, not only in our own class but also, regrettably, among the common people as well, there's scarcely one who hasn't already been married ten times, if not a hundred or even a thousand times, like Don Juan, before his marriage. (Nowadays there are, it's true, as I've heard and observed, pure young men who know and sense that this is no laughing-matter, but a great and serious undertaking. May God give them strength! In my day there wasn't one chap in ten thousand like that.) And everyone knows this, yet pretends not to. In novels the hero's emotions are described in detail, just like the ponds and bushes he walks beside; but while they describe his *grand amour* for some young girl or other, they say nothing about what has taken place in the life of this interesting hero previously: there's not a word about his visits to brothels, about the chamber-maids, the kitchen-maids, the wives of other men. Even if indecent novels of this type do exist, they're certainly not put into the hands of those who most need to know all this – young girls. At first we pretend to them that this debauchery, which fills up the lives of half the inhabitants of our towns and villages, doesn't exist at all. Subsequently we grow so accustomed to this pretence that we end up like the English, secure in the honest conviction that we are all of the very highest morality and that we live in a world that is morally perfect. The poor girls take it all very seriously. I know my own wretched wife did. I remember that after we'd got engaged I let her read my diary, so she could get some idea of the sort of life I'd been leading previously and in particular some knowledge of my last affair, which she might have found out about from other people and which I therefore considered it necessary to tell her about. I remember her horror, despair and perplexity when she learned about it and the whole thing dawned on her. I could see she was thinking of leaving me. If only she had!'

He made his sound, fell silent, and took another mouthful of tea.

6

'No, all the same, it's better the way it turned out, better the way it turned out!' he cried suddenly. 'It served me right! But that's all in the past now. What I was trying to say was that it's only the poor girls who are deceived. Their mothers know, especially the ones who've been "educated" by their husbands, they know perfectly well what goes on. And although they pretend to believe that men are pure, their actual behaviour is altogether different. They know the right bait to use in order to catch men, both for themselves and for their daughters.

'It's only we men who don't know, and we don't know because we don't want to know. Women know perfectly well that the most elevated love – the most "poetic", as we call it – depends not on moral qualities but on physical proximity and also on things like hairstyle, or the colour and the cut of a dress. Ask any experienced coquette who has set herself the task of ensnaring the attentions of a man which she would rather risk: to be accused of lying, cruelty and even of whorish behaviour in the presence of the man she is trying to attract, or to appear before his gaze in an ugly, badly made dress – and she will always choose the former. She knows that our man's lying when he goes on about lofty emotions – all he wants is her body, and so he will willingly forgive her the most outrageous behaviour. What he won't forgive, however, is an outfit that is ugly, tasteless or lacking in style. A coquette's knowledge of this is a conscious one; but every innocent young girl knows it unconsciously, as animals do.

'That's the reason for those insufferable stockinets, those fake posteriors, those bare shoulders, arms – breasts, almost. Women, especially women who've undergone the "education" provided by men, know very well that all talk about higher things is just talk, that all a man really wants is her body, and all the things that show it off in the most enticing fashion possible. And that's what they give him. You know, if only one is able to kick the habit of all this squalor that's become second nature to us and takes a look at the life of our upper classes as it really is in all its shamelessness, one can see that what we live in is a sort of licensed brothel. Don't you agree? I can prove it to you if you like,' he said, not letting me get a word in. 'You may say that women of our class act out of interests that are different from those of the women in the whorehouses, but I say that the contrary is true, and I can prove it. If people differ as regards the purpose, the inner content of their lives, that difference will inevitably be reflected in outward things, and those will differ, too. But look at those poor despised wretches, and then cast a glance at our society ladies: the same exposure of arms, shoulders, breasts, the same flaunted, tightly clad posteriors, the same passion for precious stones and shiny, expensive objects, the same diversions – music, dancing, singing. Just as the former seek to entice men by all the means at their disposal, so do the latter. There's no difference. At a rule, we may say that while short-term prostitutes are generally looked down upon, long-term prostitutes are treated with respect.'

7

'Yes, and so I fell into the trap of all those stockinets, those curls and fake bottoms. I was an easy catch, because I'd been brought up under those special conditions created for amorous young people, who are cultivated in them like cucumbers in a greenhouse. Yes, the stimulating, superabundant food we eat, together with our complete physical idleness, amounts to nothing but a systematic arousal of lust. I don't know whether you find that astonishing or not, but it's a fact. I myself had no idea of all this until quite recently. But now I can see it. And that is what I find so infuriating, that no one has any idea of what's really going on, and everyone says such stupid things, like that woman just now.

'Yes, this spring there were some peasants working on the railway embankment close to where I live. The normal food of a young peasant is bread, kvas and onions; it keeps him lively, cheerful and healthy; he works at light tasks out in the fields. He goes to work for the railway, and is fed on kasha and a pound of meat a day. But that day involves sixteen hours of labour, during which he has to trundle a wheelbarrow weighing some thirty pounds, and he soon uses up the meat. It's just right for him. But look at us: every day each of us eats perhaps two pounds of meat, game and all kinds of stimulating food and drink. Where does it all go? On sensual excesses. If we really do use it up in that way, the safety valve is opened and everything is all right. If, on the other hand, we close the safety valve, as I did mine from time to time, there immediately results a state of physical arousal which, channelled through the prism of our artificial way of life, expresses itself as the purest form of love, sometimes even as a platonic infatuation. I, too, fell in love that way, like everyone else. And it was all there: all the ecstasy, the tender emotion, the poetry. In actual fact, this love of mine was the product of, on the one hand, the efforts of the girl's mother and dress-makers, and on the other, of the excessive quantities of food I had consumed during a life of idleness. If, on the one hand, there had been none of those boat trips, those dress-makers with their waistlines, and so on, and say my wife had gone around in an ill-fitting housecoat and spent her time at home, and if, on the other hand, I had been living the normal life of a man who consumes just as much food as is necessary for him to be able to do his work, and the safety valve had been open – it happened to be closed at the time – I would never have fallen in love and none of all this would ever have happened.'

8

'Well, this time it all clicked together: my state of mind, her dress and the boat trip. And it worked. Twenty times before it hadn't worked, but now it did – the way a trap does. I'm quite serious. Marriages nowadays are set like traps. Only stands to reason, doesn't it? The girl's grown up now, she'll have to be married to someone. It all seems so simple, as long as the girl's not a freak and there are men around who want to get married. That's the way it was done in the old days. When a girl came of age, her parents arranged a marriage for her. That's how it was done, and that's how it's done all over the world to this very day: among the Chinese, the Hindus, the Muslims, among our own common people. That's how it's done among at least ninety-nine per cent of the human race. It's only we one per cent or less of debauchees who've decided that's not good enough and have thought up something new. And what is that something new? It's girls sitting in line while men come and go in front of them as if they were at a market, making their choice. As they sit there waiting, the girls think, not daring to say it out loud: "Choose me, dearest! No, me. Not her, me: look what nice shoulders and all the rest of it I have." We men walk up and down, take a look, and are very pleased with what we see. "I know what

36

they're up to," we say to ourselves, "but I won't fall into their trap." We walk up and down, we take a look, we're thoroughly gratified that all this has been arranged for our benefit. We look, are taken off our guard for a moment – and slam! There's another one caught!'

'But how do you think it ought to be?' I asked. 'Should the woman be the one to propose?'

'I honestly don't know: but if we're going to have equality, then let's have real equality. It may well be that matchmaking is a degrading business, but this is a thousand times more so. At least under the old system the rights possessed by both parties and their chances of making a decent match were equal, but nowadays a women is like a slave in a market or a piece of bait for a trap. Just you try to tell a mother or even the girl herself that all her activities are directed towards catching a husband. Dear Lord, what an insult! And yet that's all they do, and they've nothing else with which to fill their time. What's so awful is seeing even poor innocent young girls engaged in this activity. If only it were done out in the open, but no, it's all trickery, deceit. "Ah, the origin of species, how interesting! Oh, Liza's so interested in painting! And you'll be going to the exhibition? How educational! And the troika rides, and the theatre, and the symphony concert? How wonderful! My Liza's simply mad about music. Oh, do tell me why you don't share these convictions! And boating, too . . ." And all the while there's just one thought in her head: "Take me, take me, take my Liza! No, me! Go on, just for a trial!" Oh, horror! Lies!' he concluded, and, drinking up what was left of the tea, set about clearing away the glasses and the rest of the tea things.

9

'You know,' he resumed, as he put the tea and sugar away in his travelling-bag, 'it's this domination by women we're suffering from, it all stems from that.'

'What domination?' I asked. 'All the rights and privileges are on the side of men.'

'Yes, yes, that's just the point,' he said, interrupting me. 'That's exactly what I'm trying to tell you, that's what explains this curious phenomenon: from one point of view, it's perfectly correct to say that woman has been brought to the lowest degree of subjection, but from another point of view it's equally true to say that she's the dominant one. Women are exactly like the Jews, who by their financial power compensate for the oppression to which they're subjected. "Aha, you just want us to be merchants, do you? All right, then, it's as merchants that we'll lord it over you," say the Jews. "Aha, you just want us to be the objects of your sensuality, do you? All right, then, it's as the objects of your sensuality that we'll enslave you," say women. Women's lack of rights has nothing to do with them not being allowed to vote or be judges – those matters don't constitute any sort of right. No, it has to do with the fact that in sexual relations she's not the man's equal. She doesn't have the right to avail herself of the man or abstain from him, according to her desire, to select the man she wants rather than be the one who's selected. You may say that would be monstrous. Very well. Then the man shouldn't have these rights, either. The way things are at present, the woman is deprived of the rights possessed by the man. And, in order to compensate for this, she acts on the man's sensuality, forces him into subjection by means of sensuality, so that he's only formally the one who chooses – in actual fact it's she who does the choosing. And once she has mastered this technique, she abuses it and acquires a terrible power over men.'

'But where's the evidence of this special power?' I asked.

'Where? All around us, in everything. Just go into the shops of any large town. There's millions of rubles worth of stuff there; you could never put a value on the amount of labour that's gone into producing it. Yet look: in nine out of ten of those shops is there even one article that's intended to be used by men? All life's luxury articles are made in order to meet the demands of women, and be consumed by them. Just look at all those factories. By far the majority of them produce useless ornaments, carriages, furniture, playthings for women. Millions of human beings, generations of slaves perish in factories doing this convict labour merely in order to satisfy the caprice of women. Women are like empresses, keeping nine tenths of the human race in servitude, doing hard labour. And all because they feel they've been humiliated, because they're been denied the same rights men have. And so they take their revenge by acting on our sensuality and ensnaring us in their nets. Yes, that's where the trouble lies. Women have turned themselves into such effective instruments for acting on our senses that we can't even speak to them with equanimity. No sooner does a man go near a woman than he falls under her spell and loses his head. Even in my previous life I always used to get an uneasy sensation whenever I set eyes on a woman dressed in a ball-gown, but now that sight inspires me with genuine terror: I really do see in her something that's dangerous to men, something that's against all law, and I feel like calling for the police and appealing to them for protection against this danger, demanding that the hazardous object be confiscated and taken away.

'Yes, you may laugh!' he shouted at me. 'But it's no laughing matter. I'm convinced that the day will come, and perhaps before very long, when people will realize this and be amazed that there could have existed a society which tolerated actions so disturbing to public order as the ornamentation of the body, something that's so openly provocative of sensuality, yet is permitted to women in our society. It's just as if we were to set traps along all the thoroughfares men use in their daily business . . . it's even worse that that! Why is it that gambling's against the law, while women displaying themselves in prostitutes' garb that excites sensuality aren't? They're a thousand times more dangerous!'

IO

'Well, anyway, that's how I too was caught. I was what's called "in love". It wasn't just that I thought she was the acme of perfection – during the time I was engaged to her I thought I was the acme of perfection, too. After all, there's no good-for-nothing who, after looking round for a bit, can't find other good-for-nothings worse than himself in certain respects, and thus find a reason for pride and self-congratulation. That's the way it was with me: I wasn't marrying for money – material interests weren't involved as they were for the majority of my friends, who were getting married for the sake of either money or connections – I was rich, she was poor. The other thing I was proud of was that while my friends were all getting married with the intention of continuing to live in polygamy as they had done before, I had the firm intention of remaining monogamous after my wedding – and my pride in this knew no bounds. Yes, I was a dirty pig, and I thought I was an angel.

'My engagement was a brief one. I can't recall that time now without a sense of shame. What an abomination! We usually assume, don't we, that love is something spiritual, not sensual? Well, if love is spiritual, a spiritual relation, its spirituality ought to be expressed in words, in our conversations, our chats with each other. Of that there was none. Whenever we were left alone together we had a dickens of a job finding anything to say to one another. It involved a kind of sisyphean labour. As soon as you thought of anything to say, you said it – then you had to be silent again, and try to think of something else to say. There was nothing to talk about. Everything we could think of to say about the life that lay ahead of us, about our plans and our living arrangements, we had already said, and what was there left? If we'd been animals, we'd have known that talking was not what we were supposed to be doing. In this situation, however, we were supposed to talk – yet there was nothing to talk about, since what occupied our thoughts was not something that could be dealt with by means of conversation. Add to this the outrageous custom of offering each other sweetmeats, our brutish gorging on candies and desserts, and all those revolting wedding preparations: the talk about the apartment, the bedroom, the beds, the dressing-gowns, the night clothes, the linen, the toilettes. You'd agree, I think, that if people get married according to the *Domostroy*, in the manner that old man was describing, all those things like feather quilts, trousseaus and beds are just details that accompany the sacrament. But in our day, when out of ten men who get married there's hardly one who believes in the sacrament or even that what he's doing carries any particular obligation with it, when out of a hundred men there's hardly one who hasn't been married before, and out of fifty hardly one who hasn't married with the intention of being unfaithful to his wife at the first opportunity, when most men view the trip to church merely as a peculiar condition set down for their being able to possess a certain woman – think what a dreadful significance all those details acquire. In the end they turn out to be what the whole thing boils down to. It's a kind of sale: an innocent girl is sold to some debauched individual, and the sale is accompanied by certain formalities.'

II

'I got married the way everyone gets married, and the much-vaunted honeymoon began. What vulgarity there is in the very name!' he spat contemptuously. 'When I was in Paris once, I went on a tour of all the city sights; lured by a billboard, I went in to have a look at a bearded lady and a so-called "aquatic dog". The first turned out to be nothing but a man in a woman's low-cut dress, and the second a dog that had been forced into a seal-skin, swimming around in a bath-tub. It was all of very little interest; but as I was on my way out, the man in charge of the show politely followed me to the door and, when we got outside, pointed to me, saying to the people who were standing there: "Ask this gentleman if it's worth seeing! Roll up, roll up, one franc a time!" It would have pricked my conscience to say that the show wasn't worth a visit, and the man was no doubt banking on that. That's probably how it is for people who've experienced the entire beastliness of a honeymoon and who refrain from disillusioning others. I didn't disillusion anyone, either, but now I can see no reason why I shouldn't tell the truth. I even think it's necessary for the truth about this matter to be told. A honeymoon is an embarrassing, shameful, loathsome, pathetic business, and most of all it is tedious, unbearably tedious! It's something similar to what I experienced when I was learning how to smoke: I felt like vomiting, my saliva flowed, but I swallowed it and pretended I was enjoying myself. It's like the pleasure one gets from smoking: if there's to be any, it comes later on. A husband and wife have to educate themselves in this vice if they're to get any pleasure out of it.'

'Why vice?' I asked. 'I mean to say, you're talking about one of the most natural human activities there is!'

'Natural?' he said. 'Natural? No, I tell you, quite the contrary's true, I've come to the conclusion that it isn't ... natural. No, not ... natural, at all. Ask children about it, ask any uncorrupted young girl. When my sister was still very young she married a man twice her age, a thoroughly debauched character. I remember how startled we were when, on the night of her wedding, pale and in tears, she came running out of the bedroom and, trembling all over, declared that not for anything, not for anything in the world would she do what he wanted her to do – she couldn't even bring herself to say what it was.

'You claim it's natural. Eating is natural. Eating is something joyful, easy and pleasant which by its very essence involves no shame. But this is something loathsome, ignominious, painful. No, it's unnatural! And an uncorrupted young girl – of this I'm convinced – never fails to hate it.'

'But,' I said, 'how else can the human race continue?'

'Oh yes! As long as the human race doesn't perish!' he said with malevolent irony, as if he had been expecting this response as a familiar one, made in bad faith. 'To preach that one must abstain from procreation so that the English lords may continue to gorge themselves at their ease . . . that's all right. To preach that one must abstain from procreation in order to make the world a more agreeable place to live in . . . that's all right, too. But just try to insinuate that one ought to abstain from procreation in the name of morality . . . God in heaven, what an uproar will ensue! Is the human race going to disappear from the face of the earth just because a couple of dozen men don't want to go on living like pigs? But I'm sorry, excuse me. The light's getting in my eyes – do you mind if we pull the shade over it?' he said, pointing to the lamp.

I said I had no objection, and then with the haste that marked all his actions he got up on his seat and pulled the woollen shade over the lamp.

'All the same,' I said, 'if everyone thought like that, the human race would disappear.'

He did not reply at once.

'You ask how the human race would continue?' he said, settling himself down again opposite me; he had spread his legs wide apart and was leaning his elbows on his knees. 'Why should it continue, the human race?' he said.

'Why? We wouldn't exist, otherwise.'

'And why should we exist?'

'Why? So we can live.'

'But why should we live? If life has no purpose, if it's been given us for its own sake, we have no reason for living. If that really is the case, then the Schopenhauers and the Hartmanns, as well as all the Buddhists, are perfectly right. And even if there is a purpose in life, it seems obvious that when that purpose is fulfilled life must come to an end. That's the conclusion one reaches,' he said, visibly moved, and obviously treasuring this idea. 'That's the conclusion one reaches. Observe that if the purpose of life is happiness, goodness, love or whatever, and if the goal of mankind is what it is stated to be by the prophets, that all men are to be united by love, that swords are to be beaten into ploughshares and all the rest of it, what prevents it from being attained? The passions do. Of all the passions, it is sexual, carnal love that is the strongest, the most malignant and the most unyielding. It follows that if the passions are eliminated, and together with them this ultimate, strongest passion, carnal love, the goal of mankind will be attained and there will be no reason for it to live any longer. On the other hand, for as long as mankind endures, it will follow some ideal – not, needless to say, the ideal of pigs and rabbits, which is to reproduce themselves as abundantly as possible, nor that of monkeys and Parisians, which is to enjoy sexual pleasure with the greatest degree of refinement possible, but the ideal of goodness, goodness that is attained by means of abstinence and purity. Men have always striven for this ideal, and they continue to do so. But just look at the result.

'The result is that carnal love has become a safety valve. If the present generation of men hasn't yet attained its goal, that's merely because it has passions, the strongest of which is the sexual one. And since that passion exists, a new generation also exists, and thus a possibility of the goal being attained in the next generation. If this generation doesn't manage to do it, there will always be another one to follow it, and so it will continue until the goal has been attained and men have been united with one another. What would things be like if this were not the case? Imagine if God had created human beings in order to achieve a certain goal and had created them either mortal, but without the sex instinct, or immortal. If they'd been made mortal, but without the sex instinct, what would the result have been? They would have lived for a while, and failed to attain their goal; in order to achieve his aim, God would have had to create a new human race. If, on the other hand, they'd been created immortal, let us suppose (though it would be more difficult for beings of this sort to correct the error of their ways and approach perfection than it would for new generations to do so) that after many thousands of years they attained their goal . . . what good would they be then? What could be done with them? Things are still best the way they are at present . . . But perhaps you don't care for that sort of an argument, perhaps you're an evolutionist? The outcome's still the same. In order to defend its interests in its struggle with the other animals, the highest form of animal life – the human race – has to gather itself into a unity, like a swarm of bees, and not reproduce infinitely: like the bees, it must raise sexless individuals, that's to say it must strive for continence, not the excitement of lust, towards which the entire social organization of our lives is directed.' He fell silent for a moment. 'The human race disappear? Is there anyone, no matter how he views the world, who can doubt this? I mean, it's just as little in dispute as death is. All the churches teach the end of the world, and all the sciences do the same. So what's so strange about morality pointing to the same conclusion?'

He said nothing for a long time after this. He drank some more tea, put his cigarette out, and transferred some fresh ones from his bag to his old, stained cigarette case.

'I follow your meaning,' I said. 'It's a bit like what the Shakers preach.'

'Yes, and they're right,' he said. 'The sex instinct, no matter how it's dressed up, is an evil, a horrible evil that must be fought, not encouraged as it is among us. The words of the New Testament, that whosoever looks on a woman to lust after her has already committed adultery with her in his heart, don't just apply to the wives of other men, but expressly and above all to our own.'

12

'In our world it's exactly the other way round: even if a man's thoughts run on sexual abstinence while he's still single, as soon as he gets married he ceases to think it of any importance. Those trips away after the wedding, that seclusion into which the young couple retires with the sanction of their parents – all that's nothing more nor less than a licence for debauchery. But the moral law has a way of paying us back if we ignore it. No matter how hard I tried to make our honeymoon a success, nothing came of it. The whole episode was repellent, embarrassing and tedious. And it was not long before it became unbearably irksome. It started to get that way very early on. On the third day, or maybe it was the fourth, I noticed that my wife seemed to be in a listless frame of mind; I asked her what the matter was and tried to put my arms around her, thinking that was what she wanted. But she pushed me away and burst into tears. Why? She was unable to tell me. She felt depressed and ill at ease. Probably her worn-out nerves had given her an insight into the truth about the vileness of our relationship: but she couldn't express it. I continued to question her and she told me she was missing her mother. Somehow I suspected this wasn't really true. I began to reason with her, but without pursuing the subject of her

mother. I didn't realize she was just depressed, and
that this talk about her mother was simply an excuse.
But she immediately flew into a temper because I'd
passed her mother over in silence, as if I hadn't believed
what she'd been telling me. She said she could see
I didn't love her. I scolded her for being capricious,
and suddenly her face completely altered: now, instead
of depression, it expressed irritation, and she began
to accuse me in the most biting terms of cruelty
and egotism. I looked at her. Her entire countenance
expressed the most consummate hostility and coldness
– hatred, almost. I remember how horrified I was when
I saw this. "How can this be?" I thought. "Love is
supposed to be the union of souls, and now this! It
isn't possible, this isn't the woman I married!" I tried
to calm her down, but I ran up against an intransigent
wall of such cold and embittered hostility that before
I'd had time to gather my wits I was seized with irritation, and we began to say a whole lot of nasty things
to each other. That first quarrel had a terrible effect on
me. I call it a quarrel, but it wasn't really a quarrel; it
was just the revelation of the abyss that actually separated us. Our amorous feelings for each other had been
drained by the gratification of our senses, and we were
now left facing each other in our true relation, as two
egotists who had nothing whatever in common except
our desire to use each other in order to obtain the
maximum amount of pleasure. I said it was a quarrel,
what took place between us. It wasn't a quarrel, it
was just the bringing out into the open of our true
relationship, which followed upon the appeasement of

our sensual desire. I didn't realize that this cold and hostile attitude was actually the one that was normal to us, and that was because at the beginning of our life together it was very soon obscured from us by a new sublimation of our sensuality, a new infatuation with each other.

'I thought what had happened was that we had quarrelled and then made it up, and that nothing of this kind would happen again. During this same first month of our honeymoon, however, we soon reached a second stage of satiety: once again we stopped being necessary to each other, and we had another quarrel. This second quarrel had an even worse effect on me than the first one had had. "So the first one wasn't an accident," I thought. "It was bound to happen, and it'll happen again." Our second quarrel struck me all the more forcibly because it arose from the most improbable of pretexts. It had something to do with money. I've never been stingy with money, and I certainly would never have been grudging with it where my wife was concerned. All I remember is that she managed to interpret something I had said to imply that I was attempting to use my money in order to dominate her, that I'd made my money into the basis of an exclusive right over her – some absurd, stupid, evil nonsense that was unworthy of either of us. I lost my temper, and began to shout at her for her lack of tact, she accused me of the same thing, and thus it started all over again. Both in what she was saying and in the expression of her face and eyes I once again saw that cold, cruel hostility that had so shaken me previously. I remembered quarrels I had had with my brother, my friends, my father. But never had there been between us the personal, envenomed hatred that made its appearance here. After some time had passed, however, this mutual hatred was once again obscured by our 'love' – our sensuality, in other words – and once again I consoled myself with the thought that these two quarrels had been mistakes that could be made up for. But then there came a third, and a fourth, and I realized that they were no accidents, that this was how it was bound to be, that this was how it was going to be in future, and I was appalled at the prospect. I was tortured, moreover, by the dreadful thought that I was alone in having such a wretched relationship with my wife, and that everything was quite different in other people's marriages. At that stage I was still unaware that this is the common experience, that everyone believes, as I did, that theirs is an exceptional misfortune, and that everyone hides their shameful and exceptional misfortune not only from the eyes of others but also from themselves, and that they refuse to admit its existence.

'It set in right at the start of our married life together, and it continued without a break, increasing in intensity and bitterness. Even in the very first weeks I knew in the bottom of my heart that I'd been *trapped*, that this wasn't what I'd been expecting, that not only was marriage not happiness, it was something exceedingly painful and distressing. But, like everyone else, I refused to admit this to myself (I'd still not have admitted it to myself even now if the whole thing hadn't come to an end) and I hid it not only from others, but also from myself. It amazes me now that I didn't realize the situation I was in. I ought to have understood it then, for our quarrels used to start from the kind of pretexts that made it impossible, later on, when it was all over, to remember what they'd been about. Our intelligences had no time in which to lay a foundation of satisfactory pretexts beneath the increasing hostility we felt for one another. But even more remarkable were the flimsy reasons we would find for patching up our differences. Sometimes there were talks, explanations, even tears, but sometimes . . . ugh, how vile it is to remember it even now – sometimes, after we had both said the cruellest things to one another, suddenly, without a word, there would be looks, smiles, embraces . . . Ugh! What loathsomeness! How could I have failed to see the vile mediocrity of it all even then . . . ?'

13

Two passengers got on and found seats for themselves further up the carriage. He remained silent until they had seated themselves, but as soon as they were settled he continued, evidently never losing the thread of his thought for a second.

'The vilest thing of all about it,' he began, 'is that in theory love's supposed to be something ideal and noble, whereas in practice it's just a sordid matter that degrades us to the level of pigs, something it's vile and embarrassing to remember and talk about. After all, nature didn't make it vile and embarrassing for no reason. If it's vile and embarrassing, it ought to be seen as such. And yet it's quite the contrary: people behave as though what was vile and embarrassing were something beautiful and noble. What were the first signs of my love? They were that I abandoned myself to animal excesses, not only quite unashamedly, but even taking pride in the fact that it was possible for me to indulge in them, without ever once taking thought for her spiritual or even her physical wellbeing. I wondered in astonishment where this relentless animosity we felt towards each other could possibly be coming from, yet the reason for it was staring me in the face: this animosity was nothing other than the protest of our human nature against the animality that was suffocating it.

'I was astounded at the hatred we felt for one another. Yet it couldn't have been any otherwise. This hatred was nothing but the mutual aversion experienced by accomplices to a crime – both for inciting to it and for perpetrating it. What other word can there be for it but crime, when she, poor creature, became pregnant in the very first month, and yet our piglike relationships continued? Perhaps you think I'm losing the thread of my thought? Not a bit of it! I'm still telling you the story of how I murdered my wife. They asked me in court how I killed her, what I used to do it with. Imbeciles! They thought I killed her that day, the fifth of October, with a knife. It wasn't that day I killed her, it was much earlier. Exactly in the same way as they're killing their wives now, all of them . . .'

'But how did you kill her?' I asked.

'Look, this is what's really astounding: no one is willing to admit what's so clear and self-evident, the thing doctors know and ought to tell people about, instead of keeping quiet on the subject. It's so simple. Men and women are made like animals, so that carnal love is followed by pregnancy, and then by the nursing of young, both states in which carnal love is harmful for the women and her child. There's an equal number of men and women. What follows from that? The answer would seem to be quite clear. It surely doesn't require a great deal of intelligence to come to the conclusion the animals arrive at – abstinence, in other words. But oh, no. Science has managed to discover things called leucocytes that float about in our bloodstream, and has come up with all sorts of other stupid bits of useless information, yet it's unable to grasp this. At any rate, one's never heard it say anything on the subject.

'And so for the woman there are really only two ways out: one is to turn herself into a freak of nature, to destroy or attempt to destroy in herself her faculty of being a woman – a mother, in other words – so that the man can continue to take his pleasure without interruption; the other isn't really a way out at all, just a simple, gross and direct violation of the laws of nature, one that's practised in all so-called "decent" families. In other words, the woman has to go against her nature and be expectant mother, wet-nurse and mistress all at the same time; she has to be what no animal would ever lower itself to be. And she doesn't have the strength for it, either. That's where all the hysteria and "nerves" come from, and it's also the origin of the *klikushi*, the "possessed women" that are found among the common people. You don't need great powers of observation to see that these *klikushi* are never pure young girls, but always grown women, women who have husbands. It's the same in our class of society. It's equally the case in Europe. All those nerve clinics are full of women who've broken the laws of nature. But after all, the *klikushi*, like the patients of Charcot, are out-and-out cripples; the world's full of women who are only semi-crippled. To think of the great work that's accomplished in a woman when she bears forth the fruit of her womb, or when she gives suck to the child she's brought into the world. What's in the process of growing there is what will give us perpetuity, what will replace us. And this sacred work is violated – by what? It's too dreadful even to contemplate! And we carry on with our talk of freedom and women's rights. It's just as if a tribe of cannibals were to fatten up its captives before eating them, all the while assuring them of its concern for their rights and freedom.'

This was all rather original, and it made an impression on me.

'Yes, but what then?' I said. 'If that's really how it is, a man would only be able to make love to his wife once every two years, but men . . .'

'Men can't survive without it,' he chipped in. 'Once again our dear priests of science have managed to convince everyone that this is true. I'd like to see those witch-doctors compelled to perform the duties they say women must carry out as being so necessary to men, what would they have to say for themselves then, I wonder? Tell a man he needs vodka, tobacco and opium, and all those things will become necessities for him. The way they see it is that God had no idea of what human beings needed, and that he made a mess of things because he didn't consult them, the witch-doctors. You only have to take a look round to see there's something wrong. The witch-doctors have decided that men must satisfy their lust – it's a need, a necessity, and yet here are things like child-bearing and breast-feeding getting in the way. What's to be done about it? Send for the witch-doctors, they'll sort it out. And so they have. Oh, when will those witch-doctors and all their tricks be shown up for what they really are? It's high time. Now it's even got to the point where people go insane and shoot themselves, and all because of this. How can it be otherwise? The animals seem to know that their offspring assure the continuation of their species, and they stick to certain laws in this regard. It's only man who doesn't know these laws, and doesn't want to know them. He's only concerned with obtaining the greatest possible amount of pleasure. And who is this? The king of nature – man. You'll notice that the animals copulate with one another only when it's possible for them to produce offspring; but the filthy king of nature will do it any time, just so long as it gives him pleasure. More than that: he elevates this monkey pastime into the pearl of creation, into love. And what is it that he devastates in the name of this love, this filthy abomination, rather? Half of the human race, that's all. For the sake of his pleasure he makes women, who ought to be his helpmates in the progress of humanity towards truth and goodness, into his enemies. Just look around you: who is it that's constantly putting a brake on humanity's forward development? Women. And why is this so? Solely because of what I've been talking about. Yes, yes,' he repeated several times, and began to rummage about in search of his cigarettes. At last he found them and lit one, in an obvious attempt to calm himself down.

14

'So that's the sort of pig's existence I led,' he resumed, in the same tone of voice. 'And the worst of it was that, living in this filthy way, I imagined that because I didn't allow myself to be tempted by other women, I was leading a decent, married life, that I was a man of upright morality with not a stain of guilt on my conscience, and that if we had quarrels, it was her fault, the fault of her character.

'Needless to say, it wasn't her fault. She was just like all women, or the majority of them, anyway. She'd been brought up in the way the situation of women in our society demands, the way in which all upper-class women without exception are and have to be brought up. You hear a lot of talk these days about a new type of education for women. That's all hot air: women's education is exactly the way it ought to be, given the prevailing attitude towards women in our society – the real attitude, that is, not the pretended one.

'The type of education women receive will always correspond to the way men see them. After all, we know what men think of women, don't we? *Wein, Weiber und Gesang* – even the poets write things like that in their verses. Examine the whole of poetry, painting and sculpture, starting with love-poetry and all those naked Venuses and Phrynes, and you'll see that in them woman's an instrument of pleasure, just as she is on Trubnaya Street, on the Grachevka, or at the court balls. And observe the devil's cunning: if pleasure and enjoyment are what's being offered, we might as well know that there's enjoyment to be had, that woman's a sweet morsel. But that's not the way of it: from the very earliest times the knights of chivalry professed to deify woman (they deified her, but they still viewed her as an instrument of pleasure). Nowadays men claim to have respect for woman. Some will give up their seats to her, pick up her handkerchief, recognize her right to occupy any post whatsoever, participate in government and so forth. They say this, but their view of her remains the same. She's an instrument of pleasure. Her body's a means of giving pleasure. And she knows it. It's like slavery. Slavery's just the exploitation by the few of the forced labour of the many. And so, if there's to be no more slavery, men must stop exploiting the forced labour of others, they must come to view it as a sin or at least as something to be ashamed of. But instead of this, all they do is abolish the outer forms of slavery – they arrange things so that it's no longer possible to buy and sell slaves, and then imagine, and are indeed convinced, that slavery doesn't exist any more; they don't see, they don't want to see, that it continues to exist because men go on taking satisfaction in exploiting the labour of others and persist in believing that it's perfectly legitimate for them to do so. And for as long as they believe this, there will always be those who are able to do it with more strength and cunning than others. It's the same where the emancipation of woman is concerned. The reason for the condition of slavery in which woman is kept hasn't really got much to do with anything except men's desire to exploit her as an instrument of pleasure, and their belief that this is a very good thing. Well, and so they go emancipating woman, giving her all sorts of rights, just the same as men have, but they still continue to regard her as an instrument of pleasure; that's how she's brought up as a child and how later on she's moulded by public consensus. And there she is, still the same humiliated and debauched slave, while men continue to be the same debauched slave-masters.

'They've emancipated woman in the universities and the legislative assemblies, but they still regard her as an object of pleasure. Teach her, as is done in our society, to consider herself in the same light, and she will for ever remain an inferior being. Either, with the help of those sharks of doctors, she'll prevent herself conceiving offspring, and so will be a complete whore, will descend to the level, not of an animal, but of a material object; or else she'll be what she is in the majority of cases: mentally ill, hysterical and unhappy, as are all those who are denied the opportunity of spiritual development.

'Schools and universities can do nothing to change this. It can only be changed by a radical shift in the opinion that man has of woman, and that woman has of herself. That shift will only occur when woman comes to consider virginity the most exalted condition a human being can aspire to, and doesn't, as she does at present, regard it as a shame and a disgrace. As long

63

as this is lacking, the ideal of every girl, no matter how well educated, will be to attract as many men, as many males, as she can, so she can make her choice from among them.

'The fact that this one is rather good at mathematics, and that one can play the harp – that alters nothing. A woman's happy and gets everything she wants when she succeeds in bewitching a man. That's her main task in life. That's the way it's always been, and that's the way it'll go on being. A young girl in our society lives that way, and she continues to live that way after she gets married. She needs to live like this when she's a young girl so she can make her choice, and she needs to do it when she's a married woman so she can dominate her husband.

'The only thing that can put a stop to it or at least suppress it for a time is children, and then only if the woman isn't a monster, that's to say, if she breast-feeds them herself. But here again the doctors interfere.

'My wife, who wanted to breast-feed and did breast-feed our five subsequent children, had a few problems with her health after the birth of our first child. Those doctors who cynically made her undress and probed every part of her body, actions for which I had to thank them and pay them money, those pleasant doctors decided that she shouldn't do any breast-feeding, and thus throughout that early phase of our life together she was deprived of the only thing that might have prevented her from indulging in coquetry. Our child was fed by a wet-nurse – in other words, we exploited the wretchedness, poverty and ignorance of a peasant woman, and enticed her away from her own child in order to look after ours, to which purpose we dolled her up in a fancy bonnet trimmed with silver lace. But that wasn't the problem. The problem was that no sooner had she escaped from pregnancy and breast-feeding than the female coquetry that had lain dormant within her made a quite flagrant reappearance. And, every bit as flagrantly, the torments of jealousy reawoke in me: they continued to plague me throughout the whole of my married life, as they can't fail to plague men who live with their wives the way I lived with mine – immorally, in other words.'

15

'Never once, throughout all my married life, did I cease to experience the tortures of jealousy. And there were periods when I suffered particularly badly in this way. One of those periods occurred when, after the trouble with her first child, the doctors told her not to do any breast-feeding. At this time I was particularly jealous, in the first instance, because my wife was undergoing that restlessness that is characteristic of a mother and is inevitably brought on by such an arbitrary interruption of her life's natural rhythm; and, in the second instance, because when I saw with what ease she threw aside the moral obligations of a mother, I correctly, though unconsciously, drew the conclusion that she would find it just as easy to throw aside her obligations as a wife, especially since she was in perfect health and, in spite of what the dear doctors told her, subsequently breast-fed all our other children herself, and did it excellently.'

'I can see you don't like doctors,' I said. I had observed that at the very mention of them his voice acquired a peculiarly malevolent intonation.

'It isn't a question of liking them or not liking them. They've ruined my life, just as they've ruined and continue to ruin the lives of thousands, hundreds of thousands of people, and I can't help putting two and two together. I can see they're just trying to earn money, like lawyers and the rest, and I'd gladly give them half my income – anyone who understands what it is they do would gladly give them half of what they own – provided only that they shouldn't interfere with our marriages or ever come anywhere near us. I mean, I haven't got any statistics, but I know of dozens of cases – there's a vast number of them – where they've murdered the child while it was still in its mother's womb, claiming she was unable to give birth to it, and where the mother has subsequently given birth to other children without difficulty; or else it's the mothers they've murdered, on the pretext of carrying out some operation or other on them. No one even bothers to count these murders, just as no one ever counted the murders of the Inquisition, because they were supposed to be for the good of mankind. It's impossible to put figures on the number of crimes they've committed. But all those crimes are as nothing compared to the moral rot of materialism they've brought into the world, especially through woman. And all that's quite apart from the fact that if they were to follow the doctors' instructions regarding the infection they say is rife everywhere and in everything, people would have to seek not union but disunion; according to the doctors' version of things, everyone ought to keep apart from one another and never take the spray-syringe of phenol acid (which they've found doesn't have any effect, anyway) out of their mouths. But even that's not important. No, the real poison is the general corruption of human beings, of women in particular.

'Nowadays it's simply not done to say: "You're living badly, you ought to try to live better." It's not done to say that either to yourself or to someone else. If you're living badly, it's because your nerves aren't functioning properly, or something of that sort. So you have to go to the doctors. They'll prescribe you thirty-five copecks' worth of medicine, and you'll take it. You'll just make yourself worse, and then you'll have to take more medicines and consult more doctors. As a trick, it fairly takes your breath away!

'But again, that's not important. What I was trying to say was that she breast-fed her children herself, perfectly well, and that it was only her pregnancies and breast-feeding that saved me from the tortures of jealousy. If it hadn't been for that, everything would have happened sooner than it did. Our children protected both of us. In the space of eight years she had five of them. And she breast-fed them all herself.'

'Where are they now, your children?' I asked.

'My children?' he echoed, in a frightened tone of voice.

'I'm sorry, perhaps you don't want to be reminded of them.'

'No, it's all right. The children were taken into custody by my sister-in-law and her brother. They wouldn't let me have them back. I'm supposed to be a kind of madman, you know. I'm on my way home from visiting them now. I saw them, but they won't let me have them back. They think I might bring them up so they're not like their parents. And they have to be the same. Well, what can I do? Naturally they won't let me have them back, and they don't trust me. I don't even know myself whether I'd have the strength to bring them up. I think probably I wouldn't. I'm a wreck, a cripple. I've only got one thing. It's what I know. Yes, I know something it'll take other people quite a while to find out about.

'At any rate, my children are alive, and they're growing up to be the same savages as everyone else around them. I've seen them, three times I've seen them now. There's nothing I can do for them. Nothing. I'm going down south now, home. I've got a little house and garden down south.

'No, people aren't going to find out what I know for quite a while to come. If it's a question of whether there's a lot of iron or other metals in the sun or the stars, they soon get to the bottom of it; but if it's something that exposes our pigsty behaviour – they find that hard, terribly hard!

'At least you're listening to me, and I'm grateful for that.'

16

'You mentioned children just now. Again, what awful lies we spread about children. Children are God's blessing on us, children are a delight. It's all lies, you know. All that may have been true once upon a time, but it isn't nowadays. Children are a torment, nothing more. Most mothers know this, and will sometimes be quite frank about it. Most mothers in our well-off section of society will tell you they're so scared their children are going to fall ill and die, they don't want to have any, and even if they do have children, they don't want to breast-feed them in case they grow too attached to them and suffer as a result. The pleasure their baby gives them with the grace and charm of its being, of its little arms and legs, of the whole of its young body, the enjoyment they receive from their baby is not as great as the suffering they endure – not even because it falls ill or dies, but because of their fear that it may do so. Once they've weighed the advantages against the disadvantages, it seems to them that having children is disadvantageous, and therefore undesirable. They say this boldly and frankly, imagining that these feelings stem from their love of children, from a good and praiseworthy sentiment they're proud of. They don't notice that by talking like this they do nothing but negate love and affirm their own selfishness. They find less enjoyment than suffering in the grace and charm of their baby because of the fear they have for its safety, and so they don't really want this child which they are going to love. They don't sacrifice themselves for a being they love, what they do is sacrifice to themselves a being that's intended to be loved.

'It's obvious that this isn't love but selfishness. But not one hand will be raised to condemn them, these mothers from well-off families, for their selfishness, when it's remembered what agonies of suffering they go through on account of the health of their children, thanks once again to those doctors and the role they play in the lives of our better-off citizens. Even now I have only to recall the manner of my wife's existence, the condition she was in, during that early phase of our life together when she had three, then four children and was entirely absorbed in them, in order to be seized with horror. That was no life we led. It was a kind of perpetual state of danger, escape from it, then fresh danger, again followed by desperate efforts at escape, and then – another escape; constantly the sort of situation there is on board a ship that's in the process of sinking. It sometimes used to seem to me that it was all an act she was putting on, that she was just pretending to be worried about the children in order to score points over me. This way of behaving settled every problem so simply and flatteringly in her favour. It sometimes seemed to me that everything she said and did on these occasions had some kind of ulterior motive. Yet she herself suffered terribly, and constantly punished herself with guilt about the state of her children's health, about their illnesses. It was an ordeal for her, and for me as well. And she couldn't have done anything else but suffer. After all, her attachment to her children, her animal instinct to feed, caress and protect them, were just as strong in her as they are in the majority of women; she did not, however, have what the animals have – an absence of reason and imagination. The hen isn't afraid of what may happen to her chick, knows nothing of all the diseases that may attack it, or of all those remedies human beings imagine will save them from sickness and death. And the hen's chicks are not a source of torment to her. She does for them what it's natural and agreeable for her to do: her children are a delight to her. And when one of her chicks starts to show signs of being ill, the range of her concerns is very limited: she feeds the chick and keeps it warm, secure in the knowledge that what she's doing is all that is necessary. If the chick dies, she doesn't ask herself why it has died, or where it's gone, she merely clucks for a while, then stops, and goes on living as before. But that's not how it is for our unfortunate women, and that's not how it was for my wife. Quite apart from all the talk about illnesses and their treatment, about the best methods of rearing children and educating them, she was surrounded on all sides by a great mass of divergent and constantly changing rules and regulations, both printed and spoken. Children should be fed like this, with this; no, not like that, not with that, but like this; how they should be dressed, what they should be given to drink, how they should be bathed, put to bed, taken out for walks, how to see they get enough fresh air – every week we (or rather she) discovered new rules affecting all this. As if it were only yesterday that children had started being brought into the world. And if the feeding method was wrong, if the bathing was done in the wrong way or at the wrong time, and the child fell ill, then it was all her fault, as she hadn't done what she was supposed to do.

'That was if the child was healthy. And even that was torture. But just wait till it fell ill – then the fat was really in the fire. All hell would be let loose. There's a common notion that illness can be treated, and that there's a science devoted to this purpose, with people – doctors – who know all about it. Not all of them do, but the very best ones do. Right, so your child's been taken ill, and your task is to find one of those very best doctors, one who's able to save lives, and then your child will be all right; but if you can't find one of those doctors, or you don't live in an area where there is one – your child's had it. And this wasn't a faith in any way exclusive to her, it was the faith adhered to by all the women in her set, and all she ever heard from every side was: "Yekaterina Semyonovna's lost two of hers, because they didn't call in Ivan Zakharych; Ivan Zakharych saved Marya Ivanovna's eldest girl, you know. And then look at the Petrovs: they took the doctor's advice in time, he told them to get the children out of the home and they were split up and moved into various hotels and they survived – if they hadn't been separated they'd have died. And then there was that woman who had the delicate child; the doctor advised her to move down south, they did, and the child was all right." How could she have not been plagued by misery and anxiety all her life when the lives of her children, to whom she was devoted as an animal is devoted, were dependent on her being able to find out in time what Ivan Zakharych had to say? And what Ivan Zakharych would say, nobody knew, least of all Ivan Zakharych himself, since he was very well aware that he didn't really know anything at all and was quite unable to offer any kind of help, but just kept improvising blindly so that people wouldn't stop believing he did know something. After all, if she'd really been an animal, she wouldn't have suffered like that; if she'd really been a human being, she'd have believed in God, and she'd have said and thought what the peasant women say: "The Lord gave, and the Lord hath taken away; we're all in the hands of God." She'd have considered that the lives and deaths of all God's creatures, her own children included, fell outside the jurisdiction of human beings and were dependent upon God alone, and then she wouldn't have been tormented by the thought that it was in her power to prevent the deaths and illnesses of her children – but this she didn't do. The way she saw the situation was like this: she'd been given some extremely weak and fragile creatures to look after, creatures that were susceptible to an infinite number of disasters. For these creatures she felt a passionate, animal devotion. What was more, although these creatures had been delivered into her care, the means by which they could be preserved from danger had been concealed from us, but revealed instead to complete strangers, whose services and advice could only be obtained for large sums of money, and even then not always.

'The whole of the existence my wife led with her children was for her, and consequently for me as well, not a joy but a torment. How could she not have suffered? She suffered continually. We might just have calmed down after some scene of jealousy or outright quarrel and be thinking that now we'd be able to get on with our lives for a while, do a bit of reading or thinking; yet no sooner had one settled down to some task or other than the news would arrive that Vasya was being sick, or there was blood in Masha's stool, or Andryusha had a rash, and then it would all be over, life would once more cease to be possible. Where would one have to go galloping off to now, which doctors would have to be sought out, where would the child have to be taken? And then the enemas would start, the temperatures, the mixtures and the doctors' visits. No sooner would this be at an end than something else would crop up. We had no stable, regular family life. All we had was, as I've told you, a constant running battle against dangers both real and imaginary. That's the way it is for the majority of families nowadays, you know. In my own family it took a particularly nasty form. My wife was the maternal type, and she was easily gulled.

'So it wasn't just that our having children made our lives no better – it actually poisoned them. More than that: the children constantly gave us new pretexts for quarrelling. The older they grew, the more frequently they themselves were the reason for our falling out with one another; not only that – they were the weapons in a battle. It was as if we were fighting one another through our children. We each had a favourite child – a favourite weapon. My weapon was usually our son Vasya, the eldest child, while hers was usually our daughter Liza. And that wasn't all: when the children started getting a bit older and their personalities started to mature, they turned into allies whom we each tried to win over to our own side. They suffered terribly because of that, the poor children, but we were far too preoccupied with our never-ending war to pay any attention to them. The girl was on my side, while the eldest, our son, who looked like his mother and was her favourite, was often really nasty to me.'

17

'Well, that's the way we lived. We grew more and more hostile to each other. And it finally got to the point where it was no longer our disagreements that were responsible for our hostility to one another – it was our hostility that created our disagreements. Whatever she might say to me, I would disagree with it before she had even opened her mouth, and exactly the same was true of her.

'By the fourth year of our marriage we both seemed to have accepted, almost as if it had been decided for us, that we were never going to be able to understand each other or agree about anything. We'd already given up trying to settle our arguments. We each obstinately stuck to our own point of view about even the most simple things, but particularly about the children. Thinking back on it now, I can see that the opinions I used to defend were by no means so dear to me that I couldn't have got along without them; no, the point was that the opinions she held were the opposite of mine, and yielding to them meant yielding to . . . her. This I was not prepared to do. Neither was she. I think it's probable she always considered herself entirely in the right where I was concerned, and as for me, I saw myself as a saint in comparison with her. When we were left alone together we either had to remain silent or else carry on the sort of conversations I'm convinced animals have with one another. "What's the time? Bedtime. What's for dinner today? Where are we going to go? Is there anything in the newspaper? Send for the doctor. Masha's got a sore throat." We had only to stray out of this impossibly narrow focus of conversation by as much as a hair's breadth, and our mutual irritation would flare up again. Quarrels would erupt over things like the coffee, a table-cloth, a cab, or a lead at whist – none of them things that were of the slightest importance to either of us. I used to boil inwardly with the most dreadful hatred for her! Sometimes I'd watch the way she poured her tea, the way she swung her leg or brought her spoon to her mouth; I'd listen to the little slurping noises she made as she sucked the liquid in, and I used to hate her for that as for the most heinous act. I didn't notice it then, but I was regularly affected by bouts of animosity that used to correspond to the bouts of what we called "love". A bout of "love" would be followed by one of animosity; a vigorous bout of "love" would be followed by a long bout of animosity, while a less intense bout of "love" would be followed by a correspondingly shorter bout of animosity. We didn't realize it then, but this "love" and animosity were just two sides of the same coin, the same animal feeling. To live like that would have been insufferable if we'd understood the situation we were in, but we didn't understand it – we weren't even aware of it. It's the salvation as well as the punishment of human beings that when they're living irregular lives, they're able to wrap themselves in a blanket of fog so that they can't see the wretchedness of their situation. That's what we did. She tried to forget herself in a frantic round of concerns, always hastily attended to: the furniture, her clothes and those of her children, the children's health and their education. As for myself, I had my own anaesthetic, the anaesthetic of work, hunting and cards. We were both constantly busy. We both sensed that the busier we were, the more opportunity we would have for being nasty to one another. "It's all very well for you to make faces," I used to think, "but you've plagued me all night with your scenes and I've got a meeting today." "It's all very well for you," she used not only to think, but say out loud, "but I haven't been able to get a wink of sleep all night because of the baby."

'And so we continued to live, in a perpetual fog, without ever becoming aware of the situation we were in. If what finally happened hadn't happened, and I'd gone on living like that until my old age, I think that even when I was dying I'd have thought I'd had a good life, not an unusually good one, perhaps, but not a bad one either, the sort of life everyone has; I would never have come to perceive the abyss of unhappiness, the loathsome falsehood in which I was wallowing.

'We were like two prisoners in the stocks, hating each other, yet fettered to each other by the same chain, poisoning each other's lives and trying not to be aware of it. I didn't know then that ninety-nine per cent of all married couples live in the same hell I lived in, and that this can't be otherwise. I didn't know that then, either with regard to other people or with regard to myself.

'It's amazing what coincidences can take place in a life that's regularly led, or even in one that's not! Just at the point where the parents have made life intolerable for each other, an urban environment becomes necessary for the sake of the children's education. And thus the need for a move to town becomes apparent.'

For a while he said nothing, but made his peculiar noises a couple of times. Now they really did sound like stifled sobs. The train was approaching a station.

'What time is it?' he asked me.

I looked at my watch. It was two a.m.

'You're not tired?' he asked.

'No, but you are.'

'Oh, I'm just short of breath. Look, excuse me, I'm just going out for a moment to get myself a drink of water.'

And he went stumbling off up the carriage. As I sat there on my own I ran over in my mind all the things he had been telling me, and so absorbed in my thoughts did I become that I failed to notice him returning through the door at the opposite end.

18

'Yes, I keep getting led off the point,' he said when he had sat down again. 'I've changed a lot of the ideas I used to have, there are a lot of things I see differently now, and I have this need to talk about it all. Well, anyway, we went to live in town. Life's more bearable for unhappy people there. In town a man can live for a hundred years and never notice that he's long been dead and buried. There's never any time to study your conscience; you're busy all the time. There's business, social life, looking after your health, keeping up with the arts, attending to the health of your children, arranging their education. One moment you may have to receive this person, go and visit that person; the next, you may have to go and see this or that exhibition, attend this or that concert. You know how it is: at any given moment there are one, two or even three celebrities in town whom you simply mustn't miss. One moment you're taking some treatment or other, or arranging treatment for somebody else; the next, it's teachers, tutors, governesses, and yet life is as empty as it can possibly be. Well, that's how we lived, and that way we didn't feel so acutely the pain caused by the fact of our living together. More than that: in those early days we were kept busy in the most marvellous fashion, setting ourselves up in a new town, in a new apartment, with the added diversion of trips from the town to the country and back again.

'We spent one whole winter like that. During the second winter of our marriage there took place an event no one noticed at the time, one which seemed quite trivial but which lay at the root of all that was to happen subsequently. She was ill, and those reptiles had forbidden her to have any more children and had taught her a method of contraception. I found this revolting. I struggled against it, but she held firm with a frivolous obstinacy, and I yielded to her. The last excuse for our pigsty existence – children – had been removed, and our life together became even more repulsive. Even though it may be hard for him to feed them, a muzhik or a working man's children are necessary to him, and for this reason his marriage relationship has a justification. But for our sort of people children aren't necessary – they're a superfluous worry, an extra expense, co-inheritors, a burden. And the pigsty existence we lead has no justification whatso-ever. We either get rid of our children by artificial methods, or we view them as a misfortune, a conse-quence of imprudent behaviour, which is even more loathsome. There's no justification for it. But morally we've sunk so low that we don't even see the need for a justification. Nowadays the greater part of the educated classes indulges in this debauchery without the slightest shadow of remorse.

'There's no remorse left because in our section of society there's no moral conscience except the con-science – if you can call it that – represented by public consensus and criminal law. Yet neither of these are violated. There's no reason for anyone to feel guilty in the face of public opinion, since *everyone*, from Marya Pavlovna to Ivan Zakharych, does it. Why should one add to the number of paupers there already are, or deprive oneself of the possibility of leading a social life? No more is there any reason to feel guilty in the face of the criminal law or to be afraid of it. It's only whores and soldiers' wives who drown their children in ponds or throw them down wells; they, of course, should be locked up in prison, but we do it all in our own good time and without any mess.

'We lived like that for another two years. The method the reptiles had prescribed was obviously beginning to be effective; she had rounded out physically and had grown as pretty as the last ray of summer. She was aware of it, and she started to take an interest in her appearance. A kind of provocative beauty radiated from her, and people found it disturbing. She was thirty years old, in the full flower of her womanhood; she was no longer bearing children; she was well fed and emotionally unstable. Her appearance made people uneasy. Whenever she walked past men she attracted their gaze. She was like an impatient, well-fed horse that has had its bridle taken off, the same as ninety-nine per cent of our women. I could sense this, and it scared me.'

19

Suddenly he got up, moved over to the window and sat down there.

'Excuse me,' he said and, fixing his gaze on the window, sat there in silence for something like three minutes. Then he gave a deep sigh and came back to sit opposite me once more. His face had now altered completely; his eyes wore a beseeching expression, and something that might almost have been a smile creased his lips strangely. 'I'm getting a bit tired, but I'll tell you the rest of it. There's a lot of time yet; it's still dark out there. Yes,' he began once more, as he lit a cigarette. 'She'd rounded out a bit since she'd stopped having children, and that illness of hers – her constant suffering on account of the children – had begun to clear up; well, it didn't really clear up, but it was as though she'd come to after a bout of drunkenness, as though she'd recovered her senses and realized that God's world was still there with all its delights, the world she'd forgotten about and had no idea of how to live in, God's world, of which she knew absolutely nothing. "I mustn't let it slip! Time flies, and one doesn't get it back again!" I reckon that's the way she thought, or rather felt, and it was impossible she could have thought or felt any differently. She'd been brought up to believe that there was only one thing in the world worth bothering about

– love. She'd got married, she'd managed to get a bit of that love she'd been told about, but it was far from being what she'd been promised, what she'd expected, and it had brought her a lot of disillusionment and suffering; what was more, it had involved this quite unforeseen torment – children! This torment had worn her out. And then, thanks to those obliging doctors, she'd discovered it was possible to avoid having children. She'd been overjoyed, had tried the method for herself and had started to live again for the one thing she knew anything about – love. But love with a husband who was bemired in jealousy and rancour wouldn't do. She began to imagine another love that was fresh and pure – that's the way I figure it, at any rate. And then she started looking around her as though she were expecting something to come her way. I could see this, and I couldn't help feeling uneasy. Quite often it would happen that as she carried on a conversation with me through the intermediary of others – that's to say, she'd be talking to other people while really addressing herself to me – she'd come out boldly and half seriously, completely oblivious to the fact that an hour ago she'd said the exact opposite, with the statement that a mother's cares are simply an illusion, a worthless one at that, and that it's not worth sacrificing oneself for the sake of one's children when one's young and able to enjoy life. She had started to devote less attention to the children, and no longer had such a desperate attitude towards them; she was spending more and more time on herself and on her appearance (though she tried to conceal the fact), on her amusements and also her accomplishments. She took up the piano again with enthusiasm – previously she had let it go completely. That was how it all started.'

Again he gave the window a weary look. Almost immediately, however, he made a visible effort to pull himself together, and continued: 'Yes, and then this man appeared.' He faltered and made his peculiar nasal sounds a couple of times.

I could see it was torture for him to mention this man, to remember him and talk about him. But he made the effort and, as if he had tugged clear some obstacle that was in his way, he continued in a resolute tone of voice: 'He was a rubbishy fellow, as far as I could see or judge, and not because he'd acquired this importance in my life, but because he really was what I say he was. Anyway, the fact that he was so mediocre only went to prove how irresponsible she was being. If it hadn't been him, it would have been someone else, it had to happen.' Once again he fell silent. 'Yes, he was a musician, a violinist; not a professional musician, but part professional, part man of the world.

'His father was a landowner, one of my own father's neighbours. He – the father – had suffered financial ruin, and his children – he had three boys – had all found settled positions; only this one, the youngest, had been delivered into the care of his godmother in Paris. There he'd been sent to the Conservatoire, as he was musically gifted, and he'd emerged from it as a violinist who played at concerts. As a man, he was . . .' Obviously experiencing an impulse to say something bad about him, he restrained himself and said quickly: 'Well, I don't really know what sort of a life he led, all I know is that during that year he turned up in Russia, and turned up, what's more, in my own home.

'He had moist eyes, like almonds, smiling red lips, and a little moustache that was smeared with fixative; his hair was styled in the latest fashion; his face was handsome in a vulgar sort of way, and he was what women call "not bad-looking". He was slight of physique, but not in any way malformed, and he had a particularly well-developed posterior, as women have, or as Hottentots are said to have. I believe they're also said to be musical. He tried to force a kind of brash familiarity on to everyone as far as he could manage, but he was sensitive and always ready to drop this mode of address at the slightest resistance, and he never lost his outward dignity. He dressed with that special Parisian nuance: buttoned boots, brightly coloured cravats and the like – all the sort of garb foreigners adopt when they're in Paris, the sort of thing that makes an impression on women because of its distinctiveness and novelty. His manner had a superficial, affected gaiety. You know that way of talking all the time in allusions and desultory snatches, as if to say, "You know all that, you remember, you can fill in the rest for yourselves."

'He and his music were the real cause of it all. At my trial the whole thing was made to look as though it had been caused by jealousy. Nothing could have been further from the truth. I'm not saying jealousy didn't play any part at all, mind – it did, but it wasn't the most important thing. At my trial they decided I was a wronged husband who'd killed his wife in order to defend his outraged honour (that's the way they put it in their language). So I was acquitted. During the court hearings I tried to explain what was really at the bottom of it all, but they just thought I was trying to rehabilitate my wife's honour.

'Whatever her relationship with that musician was, it wasn't important to me, any more than it was to her. What was important was what I've been telling you about – my pigsty existence. It all happened because of that terrible abyss there was between us, the one I've been talking about, the terrible stress of our mutual hatred for each other that made the first pretext that came along sufficient to cause a crisis. In the last days our quarrels became terrifying; they were particularly shattering because they alternated with bouts of animal sensuality.

'If it hadn't been him, it would have been some other man. If jealousy hadn't been the pretext, some other one would have been found. I insist on the fact that all husbands who live as I lived must either live in debauchery, get divorced, or kill themselves or their wives, as I did. If there's any man alive to whom this doesn't apply, he's an extremely rare exception. You know, before I brought it all to an end in the way I did, I was several times on the verge of suicide, and she'd also tried to poison herself on several occasions.'

20

'Yes, that's the way it was, even quite a short time before it happened.

'It was as though we were living in a kind of truce and couldn't find any reason for breaking it. One day as we were talking, the subject of a dog came up. I said it had won a medal at a dog show. She said it hadn't been a medal, just a special mention. An argument began. We started to jump from one subject to another, and the accusations began to fly: "Yes, yes, I've known that for ages, it's always the same: you said . . ." "No, I didn't." "I suppose you think I'm lying!" I suddenly got a feeling that at any moment now that terrible quarrel was going to start, the one that would make me either want to kill myself or kill her. I knew it was about to begin, and I was afraid of it in the way one's afraid of a fire starting. I tried to keep myself under control, but the hatred had gained complete mastery over me. She was in the same sort of state, only worse, and she was purposely misinterpreting my every word, twisting its meaning. Everything she said was steeped in venom; she was trying to hurt me where she knew I was most sensitive. The longer it went on, the worse it got. I shouted: "Shut up!" or something like that. She went skittering out of the room and into the nursery. I tried to detain her in order to finish what I was saying and prove my point, and I seized her by the arm. She pretended I was hurting her, and she screamed: "Children, your father's beating me!" "Don't tell lies!" I shouted. "This isn't the first time he's done it!" she screamed, or something of the kind. The children went running to her, and she calmed them down. "Stop play-acting!" I said. "Everything's play-acting to you," she replied. "You'd kill someone and then say they were play-acting. Now I can see what you're really like. You actually want things to be like this!" "Oh, I wish you were dead!" I shouted. I remember the horror those terrible words filled me with. I had never thought I'd be capable of uttering such terrible, primitive words and I was amazed at the way they leapt out of me. I shouted those terrible words and then fled to my study, where I lay down and smoked one cigarette after another. Eventually I heard her going out into the hall and getting ready to go off somewhere. I asked her where she was going. She didn't answer. "Well, she can go to hell for all I care," I said to myself. I went back to my study, lay down again and continued to smoke. A thousand different plans of how I might take my revenge on her and get rid of her, making it look as though nothing had happened, came into my head. I thought about all this, and as I did so I smoked, smoked, smoked. I thought of running away from her, of hiding, of going to America. I got to the point where I dreamed that I had in fact got rid of her and of how marvellous it was going to be now: I'd meet another, beautiful woman, entirely different from my wife. I'd get rid of my wife because she'd die, or I'd get a divorce, and I thought of how I'd do it. I was aware I was getting muddled, that I wasn't thinking about the right things – but I went on smoking to stop myself being aware of it.

'But the life of the household went on as before. The governess arrived, and asked "Where's madame? When's she coming back?" The butler appeared, to ask if he should serve the tea. I went into the dining-room; the children, especially Liza, the eldest girl, who already knew what was going on, looked at me questioningly and disapprovingly. We sipped our tea in silence. She still hadn't returned. The whole evening passed, she still didn't come back, and two emotions kept alternating inside me: animosity towards her making my life and the lives of all the children a misery by her absence when I knew she intended to come back again; and fear that she might not come back, that she might do away with herself. I wanted to go and look for her. But where would I look? At her sister's? It would have been stupid to go there asking for her. Oh, let her go: if she wanted to make our lives a misery, let her make her own life miserable too. That was probably what she wanted, anyway. And next time it would be even worse. But what if she wasn't at her sister's, what if she was trying to do away with herself, or had even done so already? Eleven o'clock, twelve, one a.m. I didn't go into our bedroom, it would have been stupid to lie there alone, waiting, and I didn't want to sleep in my study. I wanted to be busy with something, write letters, read; I couldn't do anything. I sat alone in my study, suffering, angry, listening. Three a.m., four a.m.

– still no sign of her. Towards morning I fell asleep. When I woke up, she still wasn't back.

'Everything in the house continued as before, but everyone was perplexed and looked at me questioningly and reproachfully, assuming it was all my fault. And still the same struggle was going on inside me: animosity because she was making my life a misery, and worry lest anything should have happened to her.

'At about eleven o'clock that morning her sister arrived, acting as her emissary. And the usual things were said: "She's in a terrible state. What on earth have you been doing?" "Oh, it was nothing." I said something about how impossible she was, and that I hadn't done anything.

'"Well, it can't go on like this, you know," said her sister.

'"It's all up to her, not to me," I said. "I'm not going to take the first step. If she wants a divorce, we'll get a divorce."

'My sister-in-law went away empty-handed. I'd spoken boldly, on the spur of the moment, when I'd told her I wouldn't take the first step, but as soon as she'd left and I'd gone out of the room and seen the children looking so scared and wretched, I suddenly felt ready to take that first step. I would even have been glad to take it, but I didn't know how to. Once again I started to wander about the house; I smoked cigarettes, drank vodka and wine with my lunch and attained the goal I unconsciously desired: not to see the stupidity, the vulgarity of the situation I was in.

'She arrived at about three o'clock that afternoon.

She didn't say anything when we met. I thought perhaps she'd calmed down a bit, and I started to tell her that I'd been provoked by her accusations. With the same severe look of terrible suffering on her face she told me she hadn't come for explanations but in order to fetch the children; it was impossible for us to go on living together. I started to say it wasn't I who was the guilty one, that she'd driven me beyond the limits of my endurance. She gave me a solemn, severe look, and then said: "Don't say any more, you'll regret it."

'I said I couldn't bear melodramatics. Then she shrieked something I couldn't make out, and rushed to her room. I heard the sound of the key turning in her door: she'd locked herself in. I knocked, but there was no answer, and I went away in a fuming rage. Half an hour later, Liza came running to me in tears.

'"What is it? Has something happened?"

'"It's gone all quiet in Mummy's room!"

'We went to investigate. I pulled at the double door with all my might. She hadn't fastened the bolt properly, and both halves of the door opened. I went over to her bed. She was lying awkwardly atop her bed with her petticoat and her high boots still on, and she was unconscious. On the bedside table there was an empty phial of opium. We brought her round. There were more tears and, at last, a reconciliation. Yet it was not really a reconciliation: within each of us the same animosity continued to burn, mingled now with irritation at the pain this fresh quarrel had caused, pain for which each of us blamed the other. In the end, however, we had to bring it to some sort of conclusion, and life took its accustomed course. Quarrels of this kind, and occasionally even worse ones, were constantly breaking out, sometimes once a week, sometimes once a month, sometimes every day. On one occasion I even went to the lengths of getting myself a passport for foreign travel – the quarrel had been going on for two days – but then once more we had a semi-explanation, a semi-reconciliation – and I stayed put.'

21

'So that's the way things were between us when this man appeared. This man – Trukhachevsky's his name – arrived in Moscow and came to see me. It was in the morning. I asked him in. There'd once been a time when we'd been on familiar "thou" terms with one another. Now he tried, by means of phrases inserted between his use of "thou" and "you", to commit us to the "thou" form, but I put the emphasis fairly and squarely on "you", and he immediately complied. I didn't like the look of him from the very outset. But it was a strange thing: some peculiar, fatal energy led me not to repulse him, get rid of him, but, on the contrary, to bring him closer. After all, what could have been simpler than to speak to him coldly for a couple of minutes and then bid him farewell without introducing him to my wife? But no, of all things, and as if on purpose, I started to talk about his playing, saying that I'd heard he'd given up the violin. He said that, on the contrary, he was playing more than ever before nowadays. He recalled that I had been musical too, in the old days. I said that I'd let my playing go, but that my wife played the piano rather well.

'It was quite remarkable! From the very first day, the very first hour of our meeting, my attitude towards him was such as it ought really to have been only after what eventually took place. There was something fraught in my relations with him: I found a special significance in each word, each expression either of us uttered.

'I introduced him to my wife. The conversation immediately turned to music, and he offered to play duos with her. My wife was, as she always was during those last days, very elegant and alluring, disturbingly beautiful. It was obvious that she *did* like the look of him from the very outset. What was more, she was delighted at the prospect of having someone to play the violin with her – so fond of playing duos was she that she used to hire the services of a violinist from the local theatre orchestra – and her joy was written all over her face. Having cast a glance at me, however, she immediately understood the way I felt and altered her expression accordingly, and a game of mutual deception got under way between us. I smiled pleasantly, trying to make it look as though nothing could be more agreeable to me than the thought of them playing duos together. He, surveying my wife in the way all debauched men look at pretty women, tried to make it appear as though all he was interested in was the subject of the conversation, which was of course what interested him least of all. She tried to appear indifferent, but the combination of my jealous-husband look, with which she was familiar, and his lustful ogling evidently excited her. I saw that right from that first meeting her eyes began to shine in a peculiar way and that, probably as a result of my jealousy, there was immediately established between them a kind of electric current which seemed to give their faces the same expression, the same gaze, the same smile. Whenever she blushed or smiled, so did he. They talked for a while about music, about Paris, about various trivial matters. He got up to go and, with a smile on his lips, his hat resting on his thigh which from time to time gave a sudden quiver, he stood looking now at her and now at me, as if he was waiting for what we would do next. I remember that moment so well, as it was then that I could have decided not to invite him back, and then nothing would have happened. But I looked at him, and at her. "Don't think I'm jealous," I said to her mentally. "Or that I'm afraid of you," to him. And I invited him to bring his violin with him one evening and play duos with my wife. She looked at me in surprise, blushed and began to make excuses, saying that her playing wasn't good enough. This excuse-making irritated me even further, and I became all the more insistent. I remember the strange feeling I had as I looked at the nape of his neck, at its white flesh with the black hairs standing out against it, parted in the middle, as he moved away from us with his peculiar, bobbing, almost birdlike gait. I'm not exaggerating when I tell you that man's presence used to drive me out of my mind. "It's up to me to arrange things so I need never set eyes on him again," I thought. Yet to act like that was tantamount to admitting I was afraid of him. No, I wasn't afraid of him! That would be too degrading, I told myself. And right there and then in the hallway, knowing that my wife could hear me, I insisted that he should bring his violin along that very same evening. He promised to do so, and left.

'That evening he arrived with his violin and they played duos. It took them quite a while to get their playing organized: they didn't have the music they wanted, and my wife couldn't sight-read. I was very fond of music, and I took an interest in their playing, fixed his music stand for him, and turned the pages. And they managed to play a few pieces: some songs without words, and a Mozart sonata. He played excellently, with what they call a good tone. More than that: he played with a refinement and nobility of taste that were quite out of keeping with the rest of his character.

'He was, of course, a far better player than my wife, and he helped her along, at the same time managing to say nice things about her playing. He was a model of good behaviour. My wife seemed only to be interested in the music, and she behaved in a simple, natural sort of way. I, on the other hand, although I pretended to be interested in the music, spent the entire evening being tortured by jealousy.

'From the first moment that his eyes met those of my wife, I saw that the beast which lurked in them both, regardless of all social conventions and niceties, asked "May I?", and replied "Oh yes, certainly." I saw that he hadn't at all expected to find in the person of my wife, a Moscow lady, such an attractive woman, and was clearly delighting in his discovery. For there was no doubt at all in his mind that she was willing. The only problem was how to stop her insufferable husband from getting in the way. If I'd been pure, I wouldn't have understood this, but, like the majority of men, I too had thought this way about women before I'd got married, and so I could read his mind as if it were a printed book. I was particularly tormented by the fact that I could see beyond any doubt that the only feeling she had in my regard was a constant irritation, broken only by our habitual bouts of sensuality, and that this man, because of his outward elegance, his novelty and undoubted musical talent, would, as a result of the intimacy arising out of their playing together, and of the effect produced on impressionable natures by music, especially violin music, inevitably not only appeal to her, but would unquestionably and without the slightest hesitation conquer her, crush her, twist her round his little finger, do with her anything he wanted. I couldn't fail to see this, and I suffered horribly as a result. Yet in spite of this or perhaps in consequence of it, some force compelled me against my will to be, not simply extra-polite, but even kindly disposed towards him. Whether it was for my wife's sake that I did this, or for his, in order to show him I wasn't afraid of him, or whether it was in order to pull the wool over my own eyes – I don't know. All I do know is that right from the start of our dealings with each other I found it impossible to be straightforward with him. I had to be nice to him, if I wasn't to end up killing him on the spot. I regaled him with expensive wine at dinner, expressed my admiration of his playing, smiled particularly amicably whenever I spoke to him and invited him to come to our house again and play duos with my wife the following Sunday. I told him I would invite some of my musical friends to come and listen to him. And that's how it ended.'

Pozdnyshev, greatly agitated now, changed his position and made his peculiar noise.

'It's strange, the effect that man's presence had on me,' he began again, making a visible effort to remain calm. 'Coming home from an exhibition the following day or the day after, I entered the hallway and suddenly felt something heavy, like a stone, fall on my heart. At first I couldn't work out what it was. It had to do with the fact that as I'd walked through the hallway I'd noticed something that had reminded me of him. It was only when I got to my study that I was able to work out what it had been, and I went back into the hallway to make sure. No, I hadn't been seeing things: it was his overcoat. You know, one of those fashionable men's overcoats. (Though I wasn't aware of doing so at the time, I paid the most minute attention to everything that was connected with him.) I made inquiries: yes, I was right, he was here. I made for the ballroom, entering it from the schoolroom, not the drawing-room end. My daughter Liza was in the schoolroom, reading a book, and the nurse was sitting at the table with the youngest girl, helping her to spin a saucepan lid or something of the kind. The door into the ballroom was closed: I could hear regular arpeggios coming from inside, and the sound of their voices, talking. I listened, but I couldn't make out what they were saying. It was obvious that the piano-playing was meant to drown out their voices, and perhaps their kisses, too. My God! The feelings that rose up in me! I'm seized with horror whenever I think of the wild beast that lived in me during that time. My heart suddenly contracted, stopped beating, and then started again like a hammer. The principal feeling I had was the one there is in all angry rage, that of self-pity. "In front of the children, in front of the nurse!" I thought. I must have been a dreadful sight, for Liza gave me a strange look. "What should I do?" I wondered. "Go in? I can't. God knows what I might do." But I couldn't go away, either. The nurse was looking at me as though she understood my situation. "No, there's nothing for it, I'll have to go in," I said to myself, and swiftly opened the door. He was sitting at the grand piano, playing those arpeggios with large, white, arched fingers. She was standing in the crook of the piano, looking at some musical scores she had opened out. She was the first to see me or hear me, and she glanced up at me quickly. Whether she was frightened but pretending not to be frightened, or whether she really wasn't frightened at all, I don't know, but she didn't bat an eyelid, didn't even move, but just blushed, and then only after a moment or two.

'"How nice that you're back; we can't decide what to play on Sunday," she said, in a tone of voice she wouldn't have used if we'd been alone. This, together with the fact that she'd said "we", meaning the two of them, made me furious. I greeted him in silence.

'He shook my hand and, with a smile that to me seemed downright mocking, began to explain to me that he'd brought some music over so my wife could practise it before Sunday, and that they couldn't come to an agreement as to what they should play – whether it should be something more on the difficult, classical side, like a Beethoven sonata, or just short pieces. It was all so normal and straightforward that there was nothing I could find any fault with, yet at the same time I was convinced it was all a pack of lies, that they had agreed on a plan to deceive me.

'One of the most tormenting things for jealous husbands (and in our section of society all husbands are jealous) is that peculiar set of social conventions which permits the greatest and most dangerous degree of intimacy between the sexes. You'd make a laughing-stock of yourself if you were to try to prevent the kind of intimacy there is at balls, the intimacy there is between a doctor and his female patients, the intimacy that's associated with artistic pursuits – with painting, and especially music. People practise the noblest art of all, music, in pairs; the art necessitates a certain intimacy, yet there's nothing at all suspect about it – it's only a stupid, jealous husband who will see anything undesirable in it. Yet at the same time everyone knows that it's precisely these pursuits, music in particular, that cause most of the adulteries in our class of society. I'd evidently embarrassed them by the embarrassment I myself had shown. For a long time I could find nothing to say. I was like an upturned bottle from which the water won't flow because it's too full. What I wanted to do was shout at him and turn him out of the house, but once again I felt I had to be nice to him, affable to him. So I was. I made it appear as though I approved of it all, and again under the influence of that strange feeling that made me treat him all the more kindly the more unbearable I found his presence, I told him that I had the greatest confidence in his taste, and advised my wife to do the same. He stayed just long enough in order to dispel the unpleasant atmosphere that had been created by my walking into the room in silence, looking afraid – and left in the pretence that now they had decided what they would play the following evening. I, on the other hand, was fully convinced that in comparison with what was really on their minds, the question of what they were going to play was a matter of complete indifference to them.

'I accompanied him out through the hallway with especial politeness (how could one fail to accompany out a man who had arrived with the express purpose of shattering one's peace of mind and destroying the happiness of a whole family?). I shook his soft, white hand with a peculiar effusiveness.'

22

'All that day I didn't say a word to my wife – I couldn't. The mere sight of her aroused such hatred in me that I even frightened myself. At dinner she asked me in front of the children when it was I was leaving. The following week I was due to travel to the provinces to attend a meeting of the local zemstvo. I told her the date of my departure. She asked me if I needed anything for the journey. I made no reply, but sat at the table for a while in silence, and then, just as silently, went off to my study. During those last days she never came into my room, particularly at that hour. I lay there in my study, fuming with anger. Suddenly I heard familiar footsteps. And into my head came the terrible outrageous thought that, like the wife of Uriah, she wanted to conceal the sin she had already committed, and that with this purpose in view she was coming to see me in my room at this unprecedented hour. "Can she really be coming to my room?" I wondered, as I listened to her approaching footsteps. "If she is, it means I was right." And an unutterable hatred of her arose within me. The footsteps came nearer, nearer. Perhaps she would go past, into the ballroom? No, the door creaked, and there in the doorway was her tall, beautiful silhouette. Her face and eyes had a timid, ingratiating look which she was trying to conceal but which was evident to me and the meaning of which I knew only too well. I had nearly choked, so long had I held my breath, and, continuing to look at her, I grabbed my cigarette case and lit a cigarette.

'"Well, what's this? A woman comes to sit with you for a while and all you do is light a cigarette," she said, and sat down on the sofa close to me, leaning against me.

'I moved away so as to avoid touching her.

'"I see you're unhappy about me wanting to play duos on Sunday," she said.

'"I'm not in the slightest unhappy about it," I replied.

'"Do you think I haven't noticed?"

'"Well, I congratulate you for noticing. I haven't noticed anything, except that you're behaving like a flirt."

'"Oh, if you're going to start swearing like a cabby, I'd better go."

'"Go then, but just remember that even if you don't think our family's good name's of any importance, I do, and it's not you I care about (you can go to hell for all I care) but our family's good name."

'"What? *What* did you say?"

'"Just go. For God's sake go!"

'I don't know whether she was just pretending, or whether she really didn't have any idea of what I was talking about, but she took offence and flew into a temper. She got up, but didn't go away; instead she remained standing in the middle of the room.

'"You've really become impossible," she began.

"You'd wear out the patience of a saint." And trying, as always, to be as wounding as she possibly could, she reminded me of how I had behaved towards her sister (on one occasion I'd lost my temper with her sister and been rudely offensive to her; she knew that this had caused me a lot of pain, and it was here that she chose to insert her dart). "Nothing you say or do will surprise me after this," she said.

'"Yes, go on, insult me, humiliate me, drag my good name in the mire and then claim I'm the guilty one," I said to her inwardly, and suddenly I was seized by a feeling of animosity towards her more terrible than any I'd ever experienced before.

'For the first time I felt a desire to give my animosity physical expression. I leapt to my feet and went up to her; I remember that at the very moment I got up I became aware of my animosity and asked myself whether it was a good thing for me to abandon myself to this feeling, and then told myself that it was a good thing, that it would give her a fright; then immediately, instead of fighting off my animosity, I began to fan it up in myself even further, rejoicing in its steadily increasing blaze within me.

'"Go, or I'll kill you!" I shouted suddenly, going up to her and seizing her by the arm, consciously exaggerating the level of animosity in my voice. I must really have appeared terrifying, as she suddenly lost her nerve to the point where she didn't even have the strength to leave the room, but merely said: "Vasya, what is it, what's wrong with you?"

'"Go!" I roared, even more loudly. "Otherwise you'll

drive me mad, and I won't be responsible for my actions any more!"

'Having given vent to the full frenzy of my rage like this, I revelled in it, and was filled with a desire to do something extraordinary, something that would illustrate the pitch of rabid fury I had reached. I had a horrible wish to beat her, to kill her, but knew I couldn't do it, and so in order to continue giving expression to my frenzied rage, I grabbed a paperweight from my writing-desk, and with another shout of "Go!", I hurled it to the floor, narrowly missing her. I judged the shot excellently. She ran for the door, but stopped on her way out. And then without further ado, while she could still see it (I did it for her to see), I began to take other things – the candleholders, the ink-well – off my desk and threw them to the floor as well, shouting: "Go! Away with you! I won't be responsible for my actions!"

'She left – and I immediately stopped what I'd been doing.

'An hour later, the nurse came to me and told me my wife was having a fit of hysterics. I went to have a look; she was sobbing, laughing, unable to get a word out. Her whole body was trembling. She wasn't shamming – she really was ill.

'Towards dawn she calmed down, and we had a reconciliation under the influence of the feeling to which we gave the name "love".

'In the morning, when after our reconciliation I confessed to her that I'd been jealous of her and Trukhachevsky, she wasn't at all upset and burst into the most artless laughter, so strange, as she said, did it seem to her, this idea that she might be interested in a man like that.

'"Do you really think any woman with self-respect could feel anything for a man like that beyond the enjoyment of hearing him play? I tell you what, if you like, I'll never see him again. I won't even have him here on Sunday, even though all the guests have been invited now. You can write and tell him I'm not well, and that'll be that. The worst thing would be for any-one, especially him, to think that he's dangerous. And I'm far too proud to let anyone think that."

'And, you know, she wasn't lying, she really believed what she was saying. By saying this she was hoping to make herself feel contempt for him, and so protect herself from him, but she couldn't manage it. Every-thing was against her, particularly that damned music. So that's how it all ended up: on Sunday evening the guests arrived as invited, and the two of them played together again.'

23

'I think I need hardly tell you that I was very vain. In the sort of life our set leads, if a man's not vain he doesn't have much to live for. Well, that Sunday I went out of my way to see to it that the dinner and the musical evening were organized with the maximum possible good taste. I personally supervised the buying of the food for the dinner, and I issued all the invitations myself.

'By six that evening the guests had all assembled, and he appeared wearing tails and a dicky with vulgar diamond studs on it. He was behaving in a free and easy manner, replying hastily to any question that was put to him, with an understanding, acquiescent smile – you know, the kind of expression that conveyed that everything others said or did was exactly what he'd been expecting. I noted all the things that were *mauvais ton* about him now with especial satisfaction, because they helped to put my mind at rest and demonstrate to me that he was so much my wife's inferior that she would never be able, as she put it, to stoop that low. By now I'd stopped allowing myself to feel jealous. For one thing, I'd had a basinful of that particular torture, and I needed a rest; for another, I wanted to believe my wife's assurances, and so I did believe them. But in spite of not being jealous, I couldn't behave naturally towards either of them, and this was true both during dinner and throughout all the earlier part of the evening, before the music started. I kept watching their movements, their looks.

'The dinner was as such dinners usually are – tedious and artificial. The music began fairly early. Oh, how well I remember all the details of that evening. I remember how he produced his violin, the way he opened the case, removed the cloth that had been specially sewn for him by some lady or other, took the instrument out and began tuning it. I remember the way my wife sat down at the piano, trying to appear indifferent, while in actual fact she was extremely nervous – her nervousness being mostly due to fears about her own ability – and then the customary As on the piano, the plucking and tuning of the violin, the setting up of the music. Then I remember how they looked at one another, glanced round at the audience and began to play. She took the first chord. His face assumed a stern, severe, sympathetic expression and, as he gave attention to the sounds he was making, he searched the strings with careful fingers and provided a response to the piano. And so it began . . .'

He paused and made his sounds again several times in succession. He seemed to be on the point of continuing, but sniffed and paused once again.

'They played Beethoven's "Kreutzer Sonata". Do you know its first movement, the presto? You know it?' he burst out. 'Ah! It's a fearful thing, that sonata. Especially that movement. And music in general's a fearful thing. What is it? I don't know. What is music?

What does it do to us? And why does it do to us what it does? People say that music has an uplifting effect on the soul: what rot! It isn't true. It's true that it has an effect, it has a terrible effect on me, at any rate, but it has nothing to do with any uplifting of the soul. Its effect on the soul is neither uplifting nor degrading – it merely irritates me. How can I put it? Music makes me forget myself, my true condition, it carries me off into another state of being, one that isn't my own: under the influence of music I have the illusion of feeling things I don't really feel, of understanding things I don't understand, being able to do things I'm not able to do. I explain this by the circumstance that the effect produced by music is similar to that produced by yawning or laughter: I may not be sleepy, but I yawn if I see someone else yawning; I may have no reason for laughing, but I laugh if I see someone else laughing.

'Music carries me instantly and directly into the state of consciousness that was experienced by its composer. My soul merges with his, and together with him I'm transported from one state of consciousness into another; yet why this should be, I've no idea. I mean, take the man who wrote the "Kreutzer Sonata", Beethoven: he knew why he was in that state of mind. It was that state of mind which led him to perform certain actions, and so it acquired a special significance for him, but none whatever for me. And that's why that kind of music's just an irritant – because it doesn't lead anywhere. A military band plays a march, say: the soldiers march in step, and the music's done its work. An orchestra plays a dance tune, I dance, and the music's done its work. A Mass is sung, I take communion, and once again the music's done its work. But that other kind of music's just an irritation, an excitement, and the action the excitement's supposed to lead to simply isn't there! That's why it's such a fearful thing, why it sometimes has such a horrible effect. In China, music's an affair of state. And that's the way it ought to be. Can it really be allowable for anyone who feels like it to hypnotize another person, or many other persons, and then do what he likes with them? Particularly if the hypnotist is just the first unscrupulous individual who happens to come along?

'Yet this fearful medium is available to anyone who cares to make use of it. Take that "Kreutzer Sonata", for example, take its first movement, the presto: can one really allow it to be played in a drawing-room full of women in low-cut dresses? To be played, and then followed by a little light applause, and the eating of ice-cream, and talk about the latest society gossip? Such pieces should only be played on certain special, solemn, significant occasions when certain solemn actions have to be performed, actions that correspond to the nature of the music. It should be played, and as it's played those actions which it's inspired with its significance should be performed. Otherwise the generation of all that feeling and energy, which are quite inappropriate to either the place or the occasion, and which aren't allowed any outlet, can't have anything but a harmful effect. On me, at any rate, that piece had the most shattering effect; I had the illusion that I was discovering entirely new emotions, new possibilities I'd known nothing of before then. "Yes, that's it, it's got absolutely nothing to do with the way I've been used to living and seeing the world, that's how it ought to be," I seemed to hear a voice saying inside me. What this new reality I'd discovered was, I really didn't know, but my awareness of this new state of consciousness filled me with joy. Everyone in the room, including Trukhachevsky and my wife, appeared to me in an entirely new light.

'After the presto they played the attractive but unoriginal andante with its rather trite variations, and then the finale, which is really weak. Then, at the request of members of the audience, they played things like Ernst's "Elégie", and various other brief encores. These were all quite pleasant, but none of them made one tenth of the impression on me that the presto had done. They all came filtering through the impression the presto had made on me. I felt cheerful and buoyant all evening. As for my wife, I'd never seen her looking as she did that evening. Her radiant eyes, her serenity, the gravity of her expression as she played, and that utterly melting quality, the weak, pathetic, yet blissful smile on her lips after they'd finished – I saw all this, but I didn't attach any particular significance to it, beyond supposing that she had experienced the same feelings as I had, and that she, like myself, had discovered, or perhaps rather remembered, emotions that were new and unfamiliar. The evening ended satisfactorily, and everyone went home.

'Knowing that I was due to travel away for the zemstvo meeting in two days' time, Trukhachevsky told me on his way out that he hoped to repeat the pleasure of that evening when he was next in town. I took this to mean that he didn't consider it permissible to visit my house when I wasn't there, and this pleased me. It turned out that, since he would have left town by the time I was back, we wouldn't see one another again.

'For the first time I shook his hand with real satisfaction, and thanked him for the pleasure he had given me. He also said a final goodbye to my wife. Their mutual farewells seemed to me the most natural and proper thing in the world. Everything was fine. My wife and I were both very pleased with the way the evening had gone.'

24

'Two days later, having said goodbye to my wife in the best and most tranquil of moods, I went off to the provinces. In my particular district there was always an enormous amount of business to attend to, and the place had a life of its own; it was a little world apart. On each of my first two days in the district town I spent ten hours in the zemstvo headquarters. On the second day a letter from my wife was brought to me in the council chamber. I read it there and then. She wrote about the children, about our uncle, about the nurse, about things she had bought and then in passing, as if in reference to the most ordinary event, about a visit she'd had from Trukhachevsky: he'd apparently brought her the music he'd promised her and had suggested they play together again, but she had refused. I couldn't remember him having promised to bring any music: it had seemed to me at the time that he'd said a definitive goodbye, and what she described gave me a nasty jolt. However, I had so much to do that there wasn't any time to reflect about it, and it was only in the evening, when I got back to my lodgings, that I read her letter through again properly. It wasn't just the fact that Trukhachevsky had been to the house again in my absence. The whole tone of the letter seemed forced to me. The rabid beast of jealousy began to snarl in its kennel, trying to get out, but I was afraid of that beast, and I hastily locked it up inside me. "What a loathsome thing jealousy is!" I told myself. "Nothing could be more natural than what's in her letter."

'And I lay down on the bed and began to think about the matters I had to attend to the following day. I always had a lot of trouble getting to sleep when I was away at those zemstvo meetings – it also had to do with the unfamiliar surroundings – but on this occasion I managed to fall asleep almost at once. But then – you know the way it sometimes happens, that you're seized by a sort of electric shock, and you wake up? I woke up like that, with my head full of thoughts about her, about my carnal love for her, about Trukhachevsky and about the two of them making love together. I shrank inwardly with rage and horror. But I began to reason with myself. "What rubbish," I told myself. "You've got absolutely no grounds for thinking like that, nothing of the kind's happening, nor has it happened already. And how can you humiliate yourself and her by supposing such horrors? Some hired fiddler, known to be a worthless individual, suddenly taking up with an honourable woman, the respectable mother of a family, *my* wife? What an absurdity!" was what one part of me was thinking. "How could it possibly be otherwise?" was what the other part thought. "There couldn't be anything more simple or straightforward: it was for the sake of that simple, straightforward thing that I married her, for the sake of it that I've lived with her, it's the only thing about her which I actually want and which other men, including that musician, therefore also want. He's an unmarried man, in good health (I can still remember the way he used to crunch the gristle in his chop and greedily seize the rim of his wineglass in his red lips), sleek and well fed, and not merely quite without principles but obviously an adherent of certain special ideas of his own about how best to take full advantage of the pleasures that came his way. And between them they have the bond of music, the most refined form of sensual lust. What can possibly hold him back? Nothing. On the contrary, everything is drawing him in that direction. Would she be able to hold him back? I don't even know who she is. She's a mystery, just as she's always been, just as she'll always be. I don't know her. I only know her as an animal. And nothing can or should hold an animal back."

'It was only then that I began to remember the way they had looked that evening when, after they'd finished the "Kreutzer Sonata", they played some passionate little encore – I don't recall the composer – some piece that was so voluptuous it was obscene. "How could I have gone away like that?" I wondered, as I began to remember the look on their faces. "Surely it must have been obvious that everything took place between them that evening? And surely I must have seen then that there was no longer any barrier between them? Not only that, but that both of them, especially her, were experiencing a kind of shame after what had occurred between them?" I remembered how weakly, pathetically and blissfully she had smiled as I came up to the piano, how she had wiped the perspiration from her blushing face. Even then they had been avoiding each other's eyes, and it was only at supper, when he was passing her a glass of water, that they looked at each other and gave each other a little smile. With horror now I recalled those looks, those barely perceptible smiles. "Yes, it's all taken place between them," said a voice inside me, yet almost immediately another voice said something quite different. "What's come over you? That's impossible," said that other voice. I started to get a sinister feeling, lying there in the dark, and I struck a match: the little room with its yellow wallpaper suddenly filled me with a kind of terror. I lit a cigarette; you know how it is when your mind starts to spin round in the same circle of insoluble problems – you smoke. I smoked one cigarette after another, in an endeavour to cloud my intelligence and make the problems go away.

'I didn't get any sleep at all that night, and at five a.m. I decided I couldn't stand any more of this nervous tension and would go home immediately. I got up, woke the caretaker who acted as my servant and sent him off to fetch some horses. I sent a note to the zemstvo, saying I'd been called away to Moscow on urgent business and asking them to replace me with one of the other members. At eight a.m. I got into a carriage and began my journey.'

25

The guard came in and, noticing that our candle had burned down, he extinguished it without putting a new one in its place. Outside it was beginning to get light. Pozdnyshev kept silent, sighing heavily all the time the guard was in the carriage. He continued his story only when the guard had left; and all that could be heard in the semi-darkness was the rattling of the windows of the moving carriage, and the estate manager's regular snoring. In the half-light of the dawn I could no longer make out Pozdnyshev's features. All I could hear was his voice, which was growing more and more agitated, fuller and fuller of suffering.

'I had to go thirty-five versts by horse and carriage, and then after that there was an eight-hour rail journey. The conditions were just right for a carriage ride. It was frosty autumn weather, with brilliant sunshine. You know, the time of the year when the calks in the horseshoes leave their imprints on a road surface that's even, without a single rut in it. The roads were smooth, the light was bright and the air was invigorating. I really enjoyed that carriage ride. Once it had got light and I'd started my journey, I'd felt a load lift from my shoulders. As I looked at the horses, the fields, the passers-by, I forgot where it was I was going. At times I had the illusion that I was just out for a drive, and that none of what had given rise to this journey had ever taken place. And I experienced a strange joy in those moments of self-oblivion. Whenever I remembered where I was going, I would say to myself: "It'll all be clear soon enough; don't worry your head about it." Moreover, halfway through the journey there occurred an event that delayed me and proved even more diverting: the carriage broke down and had to be repaired. This breakdown was very significant, as it meant that I got to Moscow not at five p.m., as I'd planned, but at midnight, and didn't reach home until one in the morning – I missed the fast mail train, and had to take the ordinary passenger service. All the business of being towed by a cart, getting the repair done, paying the bill, having tea at the inn, chatting with the innkeeper – all that took my mind off things even further. By twilight everything was ready, and I set off once more; it was even better driving by night than it had been by day. There was a new moon, the frost was light, the road still perfect, the horses galloped, the coachman was in a good mood; I rode along, enjoying myself, because I was completely unmindful of what awaited me; or perhaps it was because I knew only too well what awaited me, and was saying farewell to the joys of life. But this tranquillity of spirit I experienced, this ability to suppress my emotions, all that came to an end when the carriage journey was over. As soon as I got into the railway coach I lost all control over my imagination: it began to paint for me, in the most lurid fashion, a rapid sequence of pictures which inflamed my jealousy, and each of which was more cynical than the last. They were all of the same thing – of what was happening there, in my absence, of her being unfaithful to me. I was consumed with rage, indignation and a kind of strange, drunken enjoyment of my own hurt pride as I contemplated these pictures, and I couldn't tear myself away from them. I couldn't help looking at them, I couldn't erase them from my mind, and I couldn't stop myself dreaming them up. But that wasn't all: the more I contemplated these imaginary pictures, the more I believed they were real. The luridness with which they appeared before me seemed proof that what I was imagining was in fact reality. It was as though some devil was inventing the most abominable notions and suggesting them to me against my will. I suddenly remembered a conversation I'd once had long ago with Trukhachevsky's brother, and I used it in order to lacerate my feelings with a kind of triumphant ecstasy, making it relate to Trukhachevsky and my wife.

'It had been a very long time ago, but I still remembered it. Once, when I'd asked Trukhachevsky's brother if he ever went to brothels, he'd replied that a respectable man wouldn't go to some dirty, loathsome place where he might run the risk of catching an infection, when it was always possible to find a respectable woman. And now his brother had found my wife. "It's true that she's not all that young any more, she's lost one of her side teeth and she's a bit on the puffy side," I imagined him thinking, "but there you are, you have to make the best of what's available." "Yes, he thinks he's doing her a favour by taking her as his mistress,"

I reflected. "And what's more, she's safe. No, that's outrageous! What am I thinking of?" I said to myself in horror. "There's nothing of that kind, nothing. There aren't even any grounds for supposing anything of that kind. After all, didn't she tell me herself that she found the very idea of my being jealous of him degrading to her? Yes, but she was lying, she's always lying!" I cried out loud – and it started again . . . There were only two other passengers in the carriage, an old woman and her husband, both of whom were very untalkative, and when they got out at one of the stations I was left alone. I was like a wild animal in a cage: at one moment I'd leap up and go to the window, at another I'd pace stumblingly up and down, willing the train to go faster; but the carriage just went on shaking and vibrating all its seats and windows, exactly like ours is doing now . . .'

And Pozdnyshev leapt to his feet, took a few paces and then sat down again.

'Oh, I'm so afraid, so afraid of railway carriages; I get stricken with horror in them. Yes, it was horrible,' he continued. 'I told myself I was going to think about something else; I'd think about the keeper of the inn, say, where I'd had tea. And immediately I saw him in my mind's eye, the old, long-bearded innkeeper with his grandson, a boy the same age as my Vasya, standing beside him. My Vasya! Now he was seeing a musician embracing his mother. What must be taking place in his poor soul? But what did she care? She was in love . . . And it all began to seethe within me again. "No, no . . . Very well," I thought, "I'll fix my mind on the hospital I inspected yesterday. And that doctor who had a moustache like Trukhachevsky's. And the way he impudently . . . They were both deceiving me when they told me he was leaving town." And again it began. All my thoughts led back to him. I suffered horribly. I suffered mainly because of my ignorance, my doubts, my ambivalence, my not knowing whether I ought to love her or hate her. So intense was my suffering that I remember that the thought occurred to me – I found it greatly appealing – that I might get out on to the track and throw myself on the rails under the train, and thus make an end of it all. Then at least I wouldn't be able to doubt and hesitate any more. The only thing that prevented me from doing this was my own self-pity, which immediately gave way to a surge of hatred for my wife. For him I felt both a strange hatred and a consciousness of my humiliation and of his triumph, but for her I felt nothing but the most terrible hatred. "I'm not just going to commit suicide and let her off that way; she's at least got to suffer a bit, and realize how I've suffered," I said to myself. At every station I got out of the train in an attempt to take my mind off it all. I saw some men drinking in one of the station buffets, and I went in and ordered some vodka. There was a Jew standing beside me. He too was drinking. He started talking to me and, willing to do anything rather than sit alone in my carriage, I accompanied him along to his grimy, smoky, third-class compartment, the interior of which was spattered with the husks of sunflower seeds. There I sat down beside him, and he droned away, telling me various anecdotes. I listened to him, but I couldn't follow what he was telling me, as I was still thinking about my own problems. He noticed this, and began to demand that I pay more attention. At that point I got up and went back to my own carriage. "I must think about it carefully," I said to myself. "Is it really true, what I suspect, and is there really any reason for me to torture myself like this?" I sat down and tried to think it over calmly and quietly; but no sooner had I done so than it all started up again: instead of following a calm, reasoned argument, my head was filled with pictures and imaginings. "Think how often I've tortured myself like this," I said to myself, as I remembered the similar attacks of jealousy I'd had previously. "Yet every time it was a false alarm. That's probably the way it'll be this time, as well. I'll find her peacefully asleep; she'll wake up, be delighted to see me, and her words and eyes will tell me that nothing's happened and that all my suspicions are groundless. Oh how good that would be!" "Oh no, it's happened that way too often, this time it's going to be different," said a voice inside me, and it started again. Yes, that was the nature of my punishment! If I'd wanted to discourage a young man from running after women, I wouldn't have taken him to a syphilis clinic, I'd have taken him into my own soul and shown him the devils that were tearing it apart! What was really so horrible was that I felt I had a complete and inalienable right to her body, as if it were my own, yet at the same time I felt that I wasn't the master of this body, that it didn't belong to me, that she could do with it whatever she pleased, and that what she wanted to do with it wasn't what I wanted. And that there was nothing I could do to stop either him or her. He was like some Vanka-Klyuchnik before the gallows, singing a song about how he'd kissed her sweet lips, and so forth. And he had the upper hand. With her there was even less I could do. Even if she hadn't been unfaithful to me yet, she wanted to, and I knew she wanted to, and that made it even worse. It would have been better if she'd actually done it and I'd known about it, so there wouldn't have been this uncertainty. I wouldn't have been capable of saying what it was I wanted. I wanted her not to want what she couldn't help wanting. It was complete and utter madness.'

26

'At the station before the terminus, after the guard had been along to collect the tickets, I got my things together and went out on to the brake-platform. My awareness of what now lay close at hand – the resolution of the entire conflict – was making me even more nervous. I was cold and my jaws started to shake so that my teeth chattered. I shuffled mechanically out of the station with the rest of the crowd, hailed a cab, got into it and set off home. As we rode along I observed the few passers-by, the yard-keepers, the shadows thrown by the street-lamps and by my cab, now in front, now behind, and thought very hard about nothing. After we'd gone about half a verst, my feet started to feel chilled, and it came back to me that I'd taken off my long woollen socks in the train and had put them in my travelling-bag. But where was my travelling-bag? Had I left it in the train? No, I hadn't, it was there. But where was my wicker trunk? It flashed into my mind that I'd forgotten all about my luggage. However, when I discovered that I still had the luggage ticket, I decided it wasn't worth going back just for the trunk, and we travelled on.

'Even though I try hard now, I can't remember the state of mind I was in at that moment. What were my thoughts? What did I want? I've absolutely no idea.

All I can remember is that I knew some terrible and very important event was about to take place in my life. Whether that important event did in fact take place because I was thinking like this, or whether it took place because I had a foreboding that it would, I don't know. It may even be that after what happened, everything that went before has taken on a gloomy tinge in my memory. The cab drove up to the porch of our house. It was one o'clock in the morning. There were several cabs standing outside the house; their drivers were waiting for fares, as there were lights in the windows (the lights were on in the ballroom and drawing-room of our apartment). Not stopping to ask myself why there might be lights on so late in our apartment, I climbed the stairs in the same expectation of some terrible event, and rang the doorbell. The door was opened by Yegor, our good, hardworking, but not very intelligent manservant. The first thing that struck my eyes was Trukhachevsky's overcoat hanging with the other coats on the coat-stand in the hallway. I ought to have been surprised, but I wasn't – it was as if I'd been expecting this. "So it's true," I said to myself. When I'd asked Yegor who the visitor was, and he'd told me it was Trukhachevsky, I asked him if there were any other visitors. '"No others, sir," he said.

'I remember the tone of voice in which he replied to me, as if he were anxious to please me and to dispel any uneasiness I might have that there might be other visitors. "No others, sir." "I see, I see," I said, as if I were talking to myself. "And the children?"

'"All well, sir, praise be to God. They're all asleep long ago."

'I could hardly breathe, and I couldn't stop the shaking in my jaws. "That means it's not the way I thought it was," I said to myself. "I used to think, 'disaster' – and yet everything would turn out to be just the same as before. It isn't like that this time; this time it's all happened, everything I used to think about and imagine, only now it isn't imaginings but reality. It's here, all of it . . ."

'I almost burst out sobbing, but the Devil immediately whispered to me: "If you go and cry and be sentimental, they'll just part quietly, there won't be any evidence, and you'll spend the rest of your life in doubt and agony." And immediately my self-pity evaporated, and was replaced by a strange feeling – you won't believe this – a feeling of joy, that now my suffering was at an end, that now I'd be able to punish her, get rid of her, give my hatred free rein. And indeed, I did give free rein to my hatred – I became a wild beast, a ferocious and cunning wild beast.

'"No, don't, don't," I said to Yegor, who was about to go into the drawing-room. "I tell you what you can do: take a cab down to the station and fetch my luggage. Look, here's the ticket. Off you go, now."

'He went along the passage to get his coat. Afraid that he might disturb them, I followed him to his little room and waited while he put his coat on. From the drawing-room, which lay through another room, voices and the sound of plates and knives were audible. They were eating, and hadn't heard the bell. "If only they don't come out now," I thought. Yegor put on his coat, which had an astrakhan collar, and went out. I opened the door for him and closed it behind him, and I felt an eerie sensation at being alone and knowing what I had to do next. How I was going to do it, I didn't yet know. All I knew was that now it had all taken place between them, that the fact of her guilt was now established beyond all question and that now I was going to punish her and bring my relations with her to an end.

'Previously I had always hesitated, and told myself: "But what if it's all untrue, what if I'm mistaken?" This time there was none of that. It had all been irrevocably settled. Without my knowledge, alone with him, at night! That showed a disregard that was total. Or perhaps it was even worse: the audacity and the insolence of her crime were intentional, and aimed at serving as a mark of her innocence. It was all quite transparently obvious. There could be no doubt whatsoever. I was only afraid that they might try to make a run for it, think up some new way of pulling the wool over my eyes, thus depriving me of my evidence and my chance of punishing her. And in order the more quickly to catch them, I crept on tiptoe to the ballroom where they were sitting, not through the drawing-room, but through the passage and the two nurseries.

'The boys were asleep in the first nursery. In the second, the nurse was stirring, on the point of waking up, and I pictured to myself what she would think when she discovered what had happened; at this notion I was seized by such self-pity that I couldn't keep my tears back, and so as not to wake the children I ran back into the passage on tiptoe and along to my study, where I threw myself on the sofa and wept out loud.

'"I'm an honest man, I'm the son of my parents, all my life I've dreamt of family happiness, never once have I been unfaithful to her . . . yet look! Five children, and she's kissing a musician because he's got red lips! No, she isn't human, she's a bitch, a repulsive bitch! Right next door to a room full of children she's pretended to love all her life. And to have written me the things she did! To throw herself into his arms so brazenly! For all I know, it may have been this way all along. Perhaps all these children that are considered mine were really sired by the manservants! And tomorrow I'd have arrived home and she'd have come out to greet me with hair done in that special way, with that twist of hers and those graceful, indolent movements" – I saw before me the whole of her loathsome, attractive presence – "and the wild beast of jealousy would have taken possession of my heart for ever and torn it to shreds. What will the nurse think, and Yegor? And poor little Liza? She already knows something. This brazenness! This lying! This animal sensuality which I know so well," I said to myself.

'I wanted to get up, but I couldn't. My heart was beating so violently that I couldn't stay standing upright. That was it, I was going to die of a stroke. She was going to kill me. That was exactly what she wanted. What did killing matter to her? Oh no, that would be doing her far too great a favour, I wasn't going to give her that satisfaction. Yes, here I was to sit, while in there they ate and laughed and . . . Even though she'd lost the first freshness of her girlhood, he wasn't going to turn his nose up at her; actually she wasn't at all bad-looking, and, most important of all, she didn't pose any danger to his precious health. "Why didn't I just strangle her there and then?" I asked myself, remembering the moment when, a week ago, I'd shoved her out of my study and then smashed things. I vividly remembered the state of mind I'd been in at the time: not only did I remember it, I now felt the same desire to smash and destroy that I'd felt then. I wanted to act. All considerations other than those related to action went abruptly out of my head. I entered that state a wild animal knows, or the state that's experienced by a man who is under the influence of physical excitement at a time of danger, and who acts precisely, unhurriedly, but without ever wasting a moment, and with only one end in view.'

27

'The first thing I did was to take off my boots. Then, in my stockinged feet, I went over to the wall above the sofa where I kept my guns and daggers hanging, and took down a curved, damask-steel poniard that had never once been used and was horribly sharp. I removed it from its sheath. I remember that the sheath fell down behind the sofa, and that I said to myself: "I'd better see I find it afterwards, otherwise it'll get lost." Then I took off my overcoat, which I'd been wearing all this time and, treading softly in my stockinged feet, made for the drawing-room.

'I crept quietly up to the door, and then suddenly opened it. I remember the look on their faces. I remember it because it gave me an excruciating joy. It was a look of terror. That was exactly what I wanted. I'll never be able to forget the expression of desperate terror that came over both their faces in the first split-second they caught sight of me. As I remember it, he was sitting at the table, but when he saw me, or heard me, he leapt to his feet and froze with his back to the cupboard. His features wore a quite unmistakable look of terror. So did hers, but there was something else there, too. If all she had done was look terrified, it's quite possible that what took place might never have happened; but in that facial expression of hers – at least

that's how it seemed to me in that first split-second –
there was also a kind of annoyance, she looked as
though she were put out at having her love-life interrupted, her happiness with him. It was as if all she
cared about now was that no one should prevent her
from being happy. These expressions stayed on their
faces only for an instant. His terrified look quickly gave
way to one that asked a question: was it going to be
possible to lie or not? If it was, then they'd better start
now. If it wasn't, then something else was going to
begin happening. But what? He threw her a question-
ing look. When she looked back at him, it seemed to
me that her expression of annoyance had turned into
one of concern for him.

'For an instant I froze there in the doorway, clutch-
ing the poniard behind my back. At that same moment
he smiled and started to say, in a tone of voice that was
nonchalant to the point of being absurd: "Oh, we were
just playing a little music together . . ."

'"Goodness, I wasn't expecting . . ." she began
simultaneously, adopting the same tone of voice.

'But neither of them managed to get to the end of
their sentences. That same rabid frenzy I had experienced a week previously once more took possession of
me. Once again I felt that compulsion to destroy, to
subjugate by force, to rejoice in the ecstasy of my
furious rage, and I abandoned myself to it.

'Neither of them managed to finish what they were
saying . . . That something else, the thing he was afraid
of, the thing that blew all their words to kingdom come
in one instant, began to happen. I rushed at her, still

keeping the poniard hidden in case he tried to stop me plunging it into her side, under the breast. That was the spot I'd chosen right from the outset. In the very moment I attacked her, he saw what I was doing, and seized my arm – something I'd never expected he'd do – shouting: "Think what you're doing! Someone help!"

'I wrenched my arm free and went for him without a word. His eyes met mine, and suddenly he turned as white as a sheet, even his lips turned pale; his eyes started to glitter in a peculiar way, and then suddenly – this was something else I hadn't been expecting – he ducked under the piano and was out of the room in a flash. I was about to rush after him, but there was something weighing me down by my left arm. It was her. I tried to pull myself away, but she hung on to me even more heavily and wouldn't let go. This unexpected impediment, her weight and the physical contact with her, which I found revolting, inflamed me even further. I was in a rabid frenzy, and I knew I must be a fearful sight, and was glad of it. I swung my left arm round as hard as I could, and my elbow struck her full in the face. She screamed and let go of my arm. I wanted to run after him, but I reflected that it would be ridiculous to run after one's wife's lover in one's stockinged feet; I didn't want to look ridiculous, I wanted to look terrifying. In spite of the terrible fury that gripped me, I was constantly aware of the impression I was making on others, and this consideration even guided my actions to a certain extent. I turned and looked at her. She'd slumped on to a *chaise-longue*; snatching with one hand at her eyes, which I'd hurt, she was observing me. In her face there was fear and hatred of me: I was the enemy. It was the kind of fear and hatred that could only be inspired by her love for another man. Yet I might still have held myself in check and not done what I did, if only she hadn't said anything. But she suddenly began to speak, as she attempted to seize the hand in which I was holding the poniard.

'"Think what you're doing! What is this? What's wrong with you? There's nothing, nothing, nothing . . . I swear it!"

'I might still have managed to put it off a little longer, but what she had just said – from which I drew quite the opposite conclusion, namely that everything *had* taken place between them – demanded a reply. And the reply had to be in keeping with the state of mind into which I'd worked myself, which was rising in a non-stop crescendo, and which could not but continue to rise. Even frenzied rage has its laws.

'"Don't lie, you repulsive bitch!" I began to yell, grabbing her arm with my left hand. But she tore herself free. Then, without letting go of the poniard, I gripped her throat in my left hand, threw her back and started to strangle her. How hard her neck was . . . She seized my hands in hers, trying to tear them free of her throat, and as if this were the signal for which I'd been waiting, I struck her with the poniard as hard as I could in her left side, beneath the ribs.

'When people tell you they don't remember what they did when they are in a mad fit of rage, don't believe a word of it – it's all lies, nonsense. I remembered everything afterwards, and I've never ceased to remember it for one second. The more steam my rage got up, the more brilliantly the light of consciousness flared within me, making it impossible for me not to be aware of everything I was doing. I can't claim that I knew in advance what I was going to do, but I was aware of each action I took at the moment I performed it, and sometimes, I think, a little before. It was as if it had been arranged like this so I could repent, so I could tell myself I was capable of stopping if I wanted to. I knew that I was striking her with the poniard under the ribs, and that it was going to go in. At the moment I did it, I knew I was doing something horrific, something the like of which I had never done before, and that it was going to have terrible consequences. But that awareness came and went like a flash of lightning, and was instantly followed by the act itself. I was blindingly aware of that act, too. I felt – I can remember it now – the momentary resistance of her corset, and of something else as well, and then the way the poniard sank into something soft. She grabbed at the poniard with both hands, lacerating them on the blade, but she couldn't stop it from going in. For a long time afterwards, in prison, when a change of heart had taken place in me, I used to think about that moment, remembering what I could of it, and weighing it up in my mind. I would remember that for a split-second – only a split-second, mind you – before I did what I did, I had a terrible awareness that I was killing, that I'd killed a woman, a defenceless woman, my wife. I remember the horror of that awareness even now, and putting two and two together I think that once I'd stuck the poniard into her, I must have pulled it out again (I even have a dim memory of doing this), in an attempt to set right what I'd done and put a stop to it all. For a second I stood without moving, waiting to see what would happen, and whether everything was going to be all right again. She leapt to her feet and screamed: "Nurse, he's killed me!"

'The nurse had heard the noise, and was standing in the doorway. I continued to stand there, waiting, unable to believe what had happened. But then suddenly the blood came gushing out from under her corset. It was only then that I realized it couldn't be put right again, and I immediately made up my mind that there was no need for it to be put right, that this was just what I'd wanted, and what I'd been obliged to do. I waited a little, until she'd fallen down, and the nurse, with a scream of "Lord Almighty!", had run to her side, and only then did I throw down the poniard and stalk out of the room.

' "It's no good getting all worked up, I must be aware of what I'm doing," I told myself, looking neither at her nor at the nurse. The nurse was screaming, calling for the maid. I stalked along the passage, and, after I'd told the maid to go and help, went into my room. "What am I going to do now?" I wondered, and immediately knew the answer to my question. As I walked into my study, I made straight for the wall, took down a revolver, examined it – it was loaded – and placed it on the desk. Then, taking care to retrieve the sheath from behind it first, I sat down on the sofa.

'I sat there for a long time. I thought about nothing, remembering nothing. Along the passage I could hear people moving about. I heard someone come into the house, followed by someone else. Then there was a noise, and I saw Yegor come into my room carrying the wicker trunk he'd fetched from the station. As if anyone needed it now!

' "Haven't you heard what's happened?" I asked him. "Tell the yard-keeper to inform the police."

'He made no reply, and went away. I got up, locked the door, found my cigarettes and matches, and had a smoke. I'd hardly finished my cigarette when sleep overcame me and rendered me senseless. I remember I dreamed that she and I were on friendly terms again, that we'd had a quarrel but had made it up; we still had a few outstanding differences, but we were friends once more. I was woken by a knocking at the door. "That'll be the police!" I thought. "After all, I've just committed a murder, I think. Or maybe it's her, and nothing has happened." There was more knocking. I didn't go to see who it was, I was trying to make up my mind whether it had all really happened or not. Yes, it had. I had a memory of her corset's resistance, of the way the poniard had sunk into her, and a chill ran down my spine. "Yes, it happened, all right," I said to myself. "And now it's my turn." But even as I silently formed these words, I knew I wasn't going to kill myself. It was a strange thing: I remembered how many times before I'd been on the point of committing

suicide; even that day in the train it had seemed easy
to me, easy because I'd thought of how it would put
the fear of God into her. Now, however, not only was
I unable to kill myself – nothing could have been
further from my thoughts. "Why should I?" I asked
myself, and there was no reply. The knocking came
again. "Right," I said to myself. "The first thing I must
do is find out who that is. I'm not in any hurry." I put
the revolver back on the desk and covered it with a
newspaper. Then I went to the door and undid the
latch. It was my wife's sister, that kind-hearted, brain-
less widow.

'"Vasya! What's happened?" she said, and the tears
she always had ready started to flow.

'"What do you want?" I asked her, rudely. I knew
there was absolutely no excuse for my being rude to
her, nor would any purpose be served by it, but I
couldn't think of any other tone of voice to adopt.

'"Vasya! She's dying! Ivan Fyodorovich said so."
Ivan Fyodorovich was my wife's doctor and adviser.

'"Is he here?" I asked, and all my hatred for her
seethed up again. "Well, what of it?"

'"Vasya, go in and see her. Oh, this is terrible," she
said.

'"Go in and see her?" I said, phrasing the words in
the form of a question to myself. And I immediately
knew the answer, knew that I must go in and see her,
that when a husband had murdered his wife, as I had
done, the correct thing was for him to go in and see
her. "If that's the correct thing to do, then I must go in,"
I told myself. "And if I have to, I'll still have time,"

I thought, apropos of my intention to commit suicide. I followed my sister-in-law out.

'"Wait," I said to her. "I'll look ridiculous without my boots, let me at least put a pair of slippers on."'

28

'And it really was quite remarkable! Once again, as I emerged from my study and passed through the familiar rooms, once again there rose within me the hope that nothing at all had happened. But then the smell of that vile stuff doctors use – iodoform, phenol acid – or whatever it is – hit my nostrils. No, it had happened all right, all of it. As I passed the nursery I caught sight of Liza. She was looking at me with frightened eyes. For a moment it even seemed to me that all five children were in there, and that they were all looking at me. I went up to her bedroom. The maid came to the door, let me in and left. The first thing that leapt to my gaze was her light-grey dress draped over a chair; the dress was stained black all over with blood. She was lying on our double bed, on my side of it (it was easier of access), her knees raised. She was lying almost supine, on a pair of pillows, and she was wearing an unbuttoned bed-jacket. Some stuff or other had been applied to the place where the wound was. There was a heavy smell of iodoform in the room. What struck me most forcibly was her face: it was swollen, and along part of her nose and under one eye it was blue with bruises. This was the result of the blow I'd given her with my elbow when she'd been trying to hold me back. She had no beauty at all now, and I felt there was something repulsive about her. I stood still on the threshold.

'"Go in, go in to her," said my sister-in-law.

'"Yes, I expect she wants to confess," I thought. "Shall I forgive her? Yes, she's dying, and so can be forgiven," I said to myself, trying to be magnanimous. I went in and walked right up to her. She looked up at me with difficulty – she had a black eye – and she said, haltingly: "You've got what you wanted, you've killed me . . ." And through all her physical suffering, her nearness to death, even, I saw displayed on her face the same inveterate look of cold, animal hatred I knew so well. "Even so . . . I won't . . . let you have . . . the children . . . She" – her sister – "will look after them . . ."

'The thing I thought most important – the question of her guilt, her unfaithfulness – she didn't even seem to think worth mentioning.

'"Yes, admire what you've done," she said, looking towards the door, and she gave a sob. Her sister was standing in the doorway with the children. "Yes, there it is, there's what you've done."

'I looked at the children, at her battered face with its bruises, and for the first time I forgot about myself, about my marital rights and my injured pride; for the first time I saw her as a human being. And so insignificant did all that had hurt me and made me jealous appear, and so significant what I'd done, that I wanted to press my face to her hand and say: "Forgive me!" – but I didn't dare to.

'She fell silent, closing her eyes, and obviously without

the strength to speak any more. Then her disfigured face began to quiver and was creased with a frown. Feebly, she pushed me away.

'"Why did all this happen? Why?"

'"Forgive me," I said.

'"Forgive? That's all nonsense! . . . If only I wasn't going to die! . . ." she screamed, heaving herself up and transfixing me with her feverishly glittering eyes. "Yes, you've got what you wanted! . . . I hate you! . . . Ah! Ah!" she cried, evidently in delirium now, and afraid of something. "Go on, kill me, kill me, I'm not afraid . . . Only kill all of us, all of us, him too. He's gone, he's gone!"

'After that, her fever became continuous. She couldn't recognize anyone any more. She died towards noon that same day. Before then, at eight a.m. to be precise, I'd been taken to the local police station and from there to prison. And there I remained for eleven months awaiting trial. During that time I thought a great deal about myself and my past life, and I grasped what it had all been about. I began to grasp it on my third day. It was on that third day that they took me there . . .'

He was about to say something else, but could not hold back his sobbing, and had to stop. Pulling himself together with an effort, he continued:

'I only began to grasp it when I saw her in her coffin . . .' He gave a sob, but continued hastily, at once: 'It was only when I saw her dead face that I realized what I'd done. I realized that I'd killed her, that it was all my doing that from a warm, moving, living creature she'd been transformed into a cold, immobile waxen one, and that there was no way of setting this to rights, not ever, not anywhere, not by any means. If you've never experienced that, you can't possibly understand . . . Oh! Oh! Oh!' he cried several times, and fell silent.

For a long time we sat there saying nothing. He sobbed and shook silently, and I looked at him.

'Well, *prostite*, forgive me . . .'

He turned away from me and lay down on the seat, covering himself up with his plaid. When we reached the station where I had to get off – this was at eight a.m. – I went over to him in order to say goodbye. Whether he was asleep or merely pretending, he didn't stir. I touched him with my hand. He threw off the plaid, and it was clear he had not been asleep.

'*Proshchayte*, goodbye,' I said, offering my hand.

He took it, and gave me the barest smile, though it was so pathetic that I felt like crying.

'Yes, *prostite*, forgive me . . .' he said, repeating the word with which he had brought his story to an end.

THE STORY OF PENGUIN CLASSICS

Before 1946 ...'Classics' are mainly the domain of academics and students, without readable editions for everyone else. This all changes when a little-known classicist, E. V. Rieu, presents Penguin founder Allen Lane with the translation of Homer's Odyssey that he has been working on and reading to his wife Nelly in his spare time.

1946 The Odyssey becomes the first Penguin Classic published, and promptly sells three million copies. Suddenly, classic books are no longer for the privileged few.

1950s Rieu, now series editor, turns to professional writers for the best modern, readable translations, including Dorothy L. Sayers's *Inferno* and Robert Graves's *The Twelve Caesars*, which revives the salacious original.

1960s 1961 sees the arrival of the Penguin Modern Classics, showcasing the best twentieth-century writers from around the world. Rieu retires in 1964, hailing the Penguin Classics list as 'the greatest educative force of the 20th century'.

1970s A new generation of translators arrives to swell the Penguin Classics ranks, and the list grows to encompass more philosophy, religion, science, history and politics.

1980s The Penguin American Library joins the Classics stable, with titles such as *The Last of the Mohicans* safeguarded. Penguin Classics now offers the most comprehensive library of world literature available.

1990s Penguin Popular Classics are launched, offering readers budget editions of the greatest works of literature. Penguin Audiobooks brings the classics to a listening audience for the first time, and in 1999 the launch of the Penguin Classics website takes them online to an ever larger global readership.

The 21st Century Penguin Classics are rejacketed for the first time in nearly twenty years. This world famous series now consists of more than 1,300 titles, making the widest range of the best books ever written available to millions – and constantly redefining the meaning of what makes a 'classic'.

The Odyssey continues ...

The best books ever written

PENGUIN CLASSICS

SINCE 1946